New Enhanced Edition *MY LIFE FOR HER*, June 2020.
First edition copyright © 2010 by Robert J. Saniscalchi.
All rights reserved. No part of this book may be reproduced, stored
or transmitted unless for review purposes.
Author: Robert J. Saniscalchi.
Editing by Matt McAvoy, Autumn Conley.

ASIN: B007TO6P6S
ISBN: 9781795673082

This is a work of fiction. Names, places, characters and incidents are
the product of the author's imagination, or are used fictitiously, and
any resemblance to actual persons, living or dead events or locales is
entirely coincidental.

MY LIFE FOR HER

A Rob and Tex Adventure

*

ROBERT J. SANISCALCHI

COMMENTS, PRAISE FROM READERS:

"This was a well-written and exciting story. The tension was dramatic and realistic; I truly could not put this book down."
J.S.MASON; a review.

"MY LIFE FOR HER is an entertaining thriller with a strong storyline. The book held my attention from beginning to end. The novel features all sorts of twists and turns, and I recommend it highly to others looking for a thrilling read."
JOHN REIZER; a review

ACKNOWLEDGMENTS

I would like to thank my friends and family for their encouragement to keep writing. Special thanks to Gloria, for her help and understanding during my long hours at the computer.

DEDICATION

This book is dedicated to those who serve in the United States military. Honor and respect for all our veterans. God bless America!

"Courage is fear holding on a minute longer."
GENERAL GEORGE S. PATTON

Chapter 1
THE NEIGHBORHOOD

Rob Marrino had sensed something odd, yet familiar; that same old feeling, that his life had circled back to the same time and place he had been once before. The day was bright, the air fresh and invigorating – he had hoped that was a sign of a new beginning; now, he had to wonder about that.

It was Rob's day off, after his first week back at work in three months. A chain of events had started in May – one he was struggling to forget. Thankfully, he was doing much better now, with the help of his doctor, his loving family and the medication.

He leaned back in his old K-Mart lawn chair, lifted the lid on his cooler and cracked open an ice-cold beer. His day's work had been carried out with passion, and now he sat admiring the mirror finish on his freshly-waxed and detailed Mustang.

Over the years, he had enjoyed working on the car, keeping it clean and tuned up. The car was a gift he had bought for himself, after making it through the bullets and bandages of the hell which was Vietnam. The 1969 Mustang, Mach 1 – in metallic red with a flat black trim –

was Rob's pride and joy, so most of the time he kept it stored safely in the garage, and drove his old, but reliable Chevy pickup.

On summer weekends, whenever they had the chance, Rob and Beth Anne – his better half – dropped the kids off at Grandma's house, then cruised on down to the shore. It was a win-win situation for everyone, because Rob's mom loved spending time with her grandchildren, and the kids loved their Grandmom – and all the goodies she made for them. Rob, meanwhile, loved to stroll along the sand dunes with Beth Anne, especially when they made their way to their little spot; their own private picnic paradise on the beach. This year, though, there were no sandy strolls; this year was all about getting back to normal, after the emotional rollercoaster of a nightmare the family had experienced.

It was a nice, warm, late-summer day, and Rob tried to put it all into perspective, attempting to think about all the good things in his life. As the doctor had wisely advised, he needed to "put the past to bed". The sky was clear blue, with a few puffy, white clouds floating by in the light breeze. What a simple pleasure it was for him to hear the birds chirping and to watch the squirrels nibbling acorns, as they scurried about the giant oak trees. Some of the summer flowers were still in bloom, and the earthy smell of freshly-cut grass wafted through the air. The warm sunshine felt good, as Rob reflected on his life since he had left the U.S. Army and bought the Mustang.

Over ten years has gone by since then, he thought. It was hard for him to believe it was 1981 already. *But, time moves on; things... change.*

Now, the Army veteran was a 31-year-old police officer, sitting in the driveway of his house in the hills of Pikesville, New Jersey, pondering life and drinking a brew. Most of the time, he felt very far away from his past; a long, long way from the jungles of Vietnam, and those bullets and bandages. Those memories had become a faint light now, nestled deep in the archives of his memory.

Unfortunately, though, on rare occasions they came back to haunt him. When they did, he could still see shadows of the faces, and feel the horror all over again. He thanked God that, as the years went by, the dreams returned less often – usually with just a glimmer of the intensity they had once held.

After the severity of the latest drama Rob and his beloved family had recently suffered, he found it surprising that he no longer dreamt at all about the ordeal. For weeks after it was over, he found himself looking over his shoulder often, fearing it could happen again; stress and sudden panic attacks had threatened to overcome him back then. Beth Anne tried to help him deal with his paranoia, but it was all she could do to care for the children and work through her own problems. Things only got worse until they went to see Dr. Harry.

Thank God we did, Rob often thought; the good doctor had really helped them to deal with their problems and settle back into life.

As for Beth Anne, she was back to her old self again, working in her garden and poring through her books. Rob now found joy in the little things, like sitting in the sunshine, listening to the birds and working on his car. His time with Beth Anne and the kids helped him stay on track. The previous Sunday, they'd all gone to church with Beth Anne's parents, and Rob realized he had missed the comfort of Father Peter's voice in those sermons; it felt good to be together, to just sit and pray.

It was a Monday afternoon, and the house and neighborhood were quiet. Rob's two children, Jennifer and little Robby, were in school, and Beth Anne was working her shift at the hospital. The children seemed to be doing fine, seldom ever mentioning those horrid happenings.

Being a cop had its benefits, if one could put up with the odd hours. Pikesville was a good place to work in law enforcement; a relatively peaceful place, with not a lot of serious crime to speak of. Rob kept busy by driving his patrol car and making his rounds around town. He also took care of occasional calls regarding emergencies, domestic problems or traffic accidents. Pikesville was a friendly little town, where everyone knew everyone. In fact, until last May, the biggest thing to happen here in years was when they lost power for two days, during the winter nor'easter. People still talked about that, and every recounting of the tale had the snow an extra few inches higher, boosted by their imagination.

It was hard for Rob to believe that it would be ten years, that autumn, since he had first joined the police force; Beth Anne's uncle, Roy, had offered him the job. Over the years, he had worked his way up the ranks and pay grade, until being promoted to sergeant, six months ago. At times, he found the work a little boring, but he liked it that way; Rob had no regrets about accepting the job.

Lord knows I paid my dues: first as the coffee and donuts deliveryman, then came that dreaded midnight shift and weekends.

Rob drained his beer, as Vietnam suddenly paid him yet another visit, along with thoughts of his old Army friends.

How are those boys doing? he wondered. *What did their lives become?*

Without his permission, his mind then drifted back to that fateful day in May.

It had begun so normally...

Rob was sitting in this same old lawn chair that day, enjoying a brew after washing his car, when his friend and neighbor hollered: "Hey, Rob, are you gonna drive that baby or just sit on your butt and stare at it all day?"

What a sight Herman was, in his baggy, slime-green shorts and a frumpy fishing hat. He was standing on his lawn with a can of Schlitz in hand and a big, stinky cigar hanging from his mouth.

Rob smiled. "Hey, meathead, when are you moving out, so I can have a big going-away party for you?"

Herman let out a big, goofy laugh. "Why would I do that

when I've got such a funny-looking neighbor to make fun of? I mean, really, man, who else just sits in his driveway, looking at his car all day?"

Herman and Rob enjoyed their banter as much as any good friends did – and at that time, Herman was still trying to get back at Rob for his latest practical joke: Rob had slopped a load of axle grease on Herman's steering wheel, and the inside door handle of his truck.

Herman had taken over his late father's plumbing business, and he kept pretty busy tending to the pipes of Pikesville. He always had plenty of cash, and he seemed to be able to choose what days he worked; he charged fifty bucks for a house call, before he had even shown up! A few years prior, Herman had offered Rob a part-time position, but the thought of fixing toilets clogged up with used Kotex and unplugging shit-filled sewer pipes had Rob refusing that idea in a hurry.

Herman lumbered over, never one to wait for an invitation. "You want a *real* beer, Rob? I know it may be a little strong for you, since you only drink that sissy light shit."

Rob had to laugh as he stood up. "Thanks, pal, but I'm about to go for a little spin; maybe pick up a few girls along the way."

Herman smiled; "Yeah, right! In your wildest dreams! Anyway, I've gotta run and get dressed; some of us around here actually work for a living. See ya later, at the game."

"Okay, Herman, whatever you say."

Rob had to laugh again as he watched his neighbor waddling back to his front door in those baggy, green shorts, leaving a stink-filled cloud of cigar smoke behind him. "See you at the game!" he yelled, as Herman went inside. Their sons were on the same little-league team, and Herman helped Rob out with the coaching, whenever he could.

Rob went into his garage and finished putting his bucket of tools away. After that, he stepped inside the house for a shower, then got dressed for a ride in the car. He had a few things to pick up for Beth Anne in town, and the errands gave him a good excuse to take a short road trip.

The Mustang roared to life and Rob waited for a few moments, satisfied by the throaty growl, as the engine warmed up. He paced the Mustang through the gears as he drove along the back roads, taking a quick but smooth ride into town. As he passed the general store, he waved at his friend and fellow police officer, Santo Mardi. After completing his wife's to-do list, and picking up a few packages at the post office, he headed north, out of town. There, he felt the rush, as he put the Mustang through the gears again, pinning himself to the seat with the incredible power of the big V-8, as he merged onto the interstate.

Loving the feel of his automobile, he decided to take a little cruise up to Mountain Pine Park. He eased back into fourth gear, and the engine smoothed to a low growl, as he accelerated to cruising speed.

He keyed his radio and called his police buddies on patrol: "Capcom, Capcom, this is Sigma. The road looks clear; no traffic. I'm going for my usual ride. Copy that?"

"Roger, Sigma, we copy: to the park and back. Have a nice trip."

That was a fringe benefit of Rob's job: the ability to drive over the speed limit without the hassle of being pulled over. In Rob's former life, he would swear he was a race-car driver, loving the feeling of high speed as he did. It helped that Uncle Roy was also the chief of police.

Beth Anne's uncle had even bought Rob a new radio, med-kit and a small strobe-light for Christmas. "A cop always has to be ready for the unexpected," he had explained. He insisted that Rob be armed at all times, when he was out on the road, so a 9mm Browning was stashed underneath the Mustang's passenger seat. Of course, Rob prayed that he would never really have to use it.

Chapter 2
BUSTED

Rob was cruising now, enjoying The Rolling Stones on his eight-track tape player, when he heard a faint but familiar sound, coming from behind him. He lowered the volume immediately, as he recognized the blaring of a police siren, growing louder as it headed his way. Following protocol, he pulled over to the right lane, then slowed. A check in his rearview revealed the flashing lights, now directly behind him.

He turned for a quick look, as a small, black, foreign car blurred past him at ridiculously high speed, followed by another blur of color, as the state police followed in hot pursuit.

"Capcom, Capcom, this is Sigma. Copy?" Rob said into his radio. "We've got a high-speed pursuit in progress; state police are tracking a small, black sports sedan. Vehicles are westbound on I-80, just past mile marker 42. I am going to assist. Copy?"

After a moment, Capcom replied: "We copy that, Sigma. We just received word that the troopers are in pursuit of drug suspects. Be advised: they may be armed. Backup is on the way."

Rob put some serious toe on the gas, and the big V-8

answered with a roar. The car lunged forward, its tires screeching, and the g-force from incredible acceleration smacked his back against the seat again, as he raced after the sedan and the cruiser. As he focused on the road ahead, eager to close the gap, adrenalin rushed through him.

Mile marker after mile marker flew by, the background a blur, as he pushed the Mustang to speeds well above 120 miles per hour. It wasn't long before he could see the cars in the distance, and he did his best to rapidly close the gap.

As he neared, he gasped at the sight of something jutting out of the passenger window of the suspects' car. *Oh my God! Is that... a rifle barrel?*

The muzzle flashes confirmed his fears; the perpetrators were firing at the troopers.

As the state police car braked and swerved, Rob was overcome by that strange feeling: the nervous but exciting sensation of giving chase. He continued past the disabled police car, in hot pursuit of the bad guys, albeit at a much safer distance.

Rob throttled the Mustang around a sharp turn, when he noticed smoke billowing from the side of the road, up ahead. As he slowed and drove closer, he could barely make out the back end of the black sports car, in the tree line. He braked hard and downshifted, stopping well off the shoulder of the road, a hundred yards past the suspects' car.

"Capcom, Capcom, this is Sigma," Rob said into his radio, trying to remain calm and focused. "Suspects are stopped on I-80, at mile marker 45, westbound; they've crashed on the side of the road. I can confirm that they are armed; there was gunfire; possible wounded in the patrol car in pursuit. Copy?"

"Copy that, Sigma: westbound marker 45. Please hold your position; backup is en route."

Rob cautiously exited his car, keeping his eyes on the smashed guardrail and the smoke drifting out over the road. It appeared that the suspects had lost control of their vehicle and smashed through, ending up about seventy-five-yards deep in the thick brush and trees. Rob grabbed his Browning, checked the clip, and instinctively headed into the roadside cover. As he approached, he slipped the pistol out of its holster and chambered a round. Then, he clicked off the safety and moved in a little closer, for a better look. Slowly, he climbed over the dilapidated guardrail, then crawled through the tall grass.

He was close to the top of a small rise. He stayed low in the cover, moving into position as carefully and quietly as possible; there, he took advantage of the cover provided by tall pines. He heard no one, nor did he see any movement, other than smoke drifting through the trees.

At that moment, the police car came to a screeching stop, directly behind him out on the roadway, its windscreen blown out. Two troopers jumped out to examine Rob's car, then scrambled to check their weapons.

"Here," Rob said, waving them over.

They looked his way and hurried toward him, with guns at the ready.

"Officer Robert Marrino, Pikesville Police," Rob quickly announced, holding up his badge; "the Mustang's mine. I saw them shooting at you; thank God you guys are alright. I called it in; backup's on the way."

"Yeah, thanks Marrino," the tall one replied, as he wiped the blood from a nasty-looking gash over his eye. "Officers Andrews and Cruz."

After he and his partner had offered handshakes, the trooper continued: "I think we're alright, except for a little windshield shrapnel in my forehead. We called it in as well." He paused to pump another round into the chamber of his shotgun.

"Now, it's payback time! There's two of 'em out there; let's go see where the hell those creeps are, and what they're up to."

"Okay," Rob replied, "but keep it low and slow, and take advantage of the natural cover; we know they're armed."

As they crawled into the smoky mist and pines, Rob heard someone yelling out in a foreign language. With the two officers behind him, he crawled a little closer, until he could just make out the back of the car. It had flipped over and was lodged against a large oak tree, still smoldering. Then, out of nowhere, one of the suspects came into view.

The man appeared to be helping his partner out of the wreckage. When he had done so, he ran to the trunk and pulled out a few large bags, slinging them over his shoulder. As well as the bags, he was carrying what looked like an AK-47 assault rifle.

"We can take 'em if they come our way," Officer Cruz whispered.

"We should focus on the one with the rifle," Rob replied; "the other one looks pretty banged up. Be careful, though, he might have a weapon as well."

As they watched and waited, ready to make their move, Rob felt a familiar fear and anxiety creeping into him; his hands trembled as he checked the safety on the Browning.

The silence was short-lived. In a flurry of sudden noise and movement, backup arrived, tires screeching and sirens blaring. At that, all hell broke loose, as the suspects turned and fired wildly.

"Down!" Rob said to the officers, and they dropped behind the pines.

Rob hugged the earth as AK-47 rounds zipped and popped overhead. For a moment, his mind drifted back in time, to the battlefields of Vietnam. He tried to stay present, in the moment, but the all-too-familiar fear and excitement of the firefight sent adrenalin coursing through him.

"Cruz? You there?" someone from backup called on the radio.

"Check your fire!" Cruz yelled. "Hold your position; we're comin' out to meet you."

After a while, the suspects stopped spending ammo, and Rob saw them holding up behind the car. He motioned for the troopers to use that moment and crawl back through the pines, toward the road.

"Rob!" Chief Roy was there; he grabbed Rob's hand the

moment he came into view. "What the hell's going on?"

Rob pointed: "I wouldn't order anyone past that rise; those guys have at least one, maybe two AK-47s. They're hiding down behind the car."

"Right, we'll be careful," Roy replied; "we don't need a death count here."

He gathered his troops, borrowed Cruz's radio and announced his plan for them to circle the suspects. "Ranger One, this is Sigma Two," Roy then said into the radio, addressing the state police captain. "We've had heavy gunfire from two heavily-armed suspects; one possibly wounded. The road is blocked off at marker 45. We need you to move to their rear, at Highway 34, and cut them off if they try to back out on us; we'll make our move from marker 45. Copy?"

After a moment, Ranger 1 replied: "Roger that, Sigma Two: Highway 34. We're moving into position."

Everyone got ready to go; Chief Roy ordered one of the troopers to stay with the cars and watch the road, then turned to Rob. "Here," Roy said, handing Rob the shotgun he kept in his car, which was loaded with magnum buckshot. Rob thanked him as he took the weapon.

The seven of them then started their slow crawl around the trees, keeping their eyes peeled. The evergreens served as protective sentries, camouflaging them as Roy scanned the area with his field glasses. When he saw the wrecked car, but no suspects, he gestured his team to move closer, then lie in wait.

"We're in position at 34," Ranger 1 said, on Roy's radio.

"Copy that," Roy said. But, almost before he had got the words out, they heard movement.

"They're on the run, boys!" Roy said, pointing at the suspects, as they hurried to take cover and move back out on the road. With their guns at the ready, the team waited for them to move closer. Then, as the suspects came over the rise, Roy yelled: "Stop right there! Drop your weapons!"

The suspects took a step back, their eyes wide and darting about, like terrified rats caught in a trap.

Rob dropped to one knee and leveled his shotgun. "Drop your weapons and get your hands up!"

The team had the bad guys dead to rights, yet still the taller adversary, carrying the bags, leveled his weapons on the police; the team was justified to open fire. They unleashed on instinct and at will; the impact from the barrage of bullets knocked the man off his feet, although he managed to fire a few wild bursts from his weapon before hitting the ground.

Rob pumped another round into the chamber and focused on the other suspect. But, there was no need to open fire again; the wounded man knew he was had, and he dropped his gun. The team moved in and grabbed him.

After checking the bloody body on the ground for a pulse which he could not feel, Rob said: "This one's gone; not breathing." He stood up and sighed, looking down at the lifeless culprit. "Guess we've got a death toll after all."

Roy came over and put a supportive hand on Rob's

shoulder. "It's okay, son: we did what we had to do; they left us no choice. Come on, I want you to take a look at our wounded prisoner, Doc; maybe you can do something for him until the ambulance gets here."

The man on the stretcher was yelling in his foreign tongue, which Rob presumed was Spanish, as he cried out in agony from the wound on his leg; Officers Cruz and Andrews fought to hold him down. Rob couldn't help but relive the war all over again, as he ran to fetch the medical kit from his car: *All those bullets; all those bandages.*

"Good job, men," Chief Roy said, with exhilaration. "Keep that one chained up with his good leg and wrist locks, after Rob has finished with him."

Rob cut the suspect's pants leg to get a better visual on the damage. The limb was badly fractured and bleeding profusely. He put a pressure bandage on it, wrapping it tightly – this caused the man to pull backward, crying out even louder. Rob pulled open the suspect's shirt, to check him for bullet wounds, but found none. "Look like the damage was just the leg injury from the collision," he told the chief; "he wasn't hit." He removed his bloodied gloves, and tried to calm his trembling hands.

The rest of the team rallied to secure the area and gather evidence. The large bags in the dead man's possession were heavy – about seventy-five pounds apiece. Looking inside revealed them to be filled with hundreds of plastic wraps of fine white powder – most likely heroin or cocaine.

More state police arrived on the scene, along with a C.S.I.

unit and E.M.S. Among the red and blue flashing lights, and the whirring of the sirens, a tow truck showed up to pull the car wreckage out of the woods. As paramedics, officers and investigators swarmed the area, there were probably more people than had ever set foot in that spot before.

Of course, the media also turned up, and a herd of reporters began shouting questions at anyone who dared to make eye contact with them, especially the police and the chief. A camera operator began taking video of the scene. The E.M.S. crews carried a zipped-up body-bag and the wounded suspect out of the woods; on a stretcher, they rolled the suspect into the ambulance, to be escorted to hospital, accompanied by Officer Cruz.

"Follow me back?" the chief asked Rob.

"Sure," Rob said, jumping into his Mustang.

On the ride back to town, Rob realized that he needed to get in touch with Beth Anne, and let her know what had happened.

When he arrived at the station, it was already immersed in commotion, and the local news crew was asking all sorts of questions, as they tried to get the scoop. Rob let Roy do all the talking, as he went inside to call Beth Anne.

He explained all about the bust to her, but did his best not to get into any of the bloody details; he didn't want to upset her.

"I'm just glad you're okay," Beth Anne said. "Just come home as soon as possible, honey."

"I will," he promised.

Making his way into Roy's office, Rob grabbed some coffee and a couple of donuts – the police buffet cliché; the sugar and caffeine would do him good. It would be hours before he was finished up with Roy, the state police and the piles of paperwork which had to be completed.

*

Just after ten p.m., Rob finally pulled into his driveway, longing for the peace and quiet of home, and for Beth Anne's company. She had sounded okay when he called, but he knew that she would be anxious to see him. It was good to see the light from the bedroom window still on, as he parked in the driveway.

When he walked inside, Beth Anne was standing in the kitchen, with that old worried look in her eyes. "Rob, what the hell happened out there? It's supposed to be your day off."

They held each other and, for a moment, Rob lost himself in the warmth of her embrace. "Please don't worry; everything's fine," he said. "I was just taking a little drive and happened to end up in a car chase, and a dangerous situation with some very bad people: drug dealers."

"Drug dealers?!" she said, with a gasp.

"Yes, but we arrested them and, thank God, none of us were injured. I'll tell you all about it in the morning; I'm beat."

She held him tightly. "'Thank God' is right, Rob! I love

you so much; I don't know what I would do without you."

Rob looked into her warm, green eyes. "You don't have to worry about it: I'm not going anywhere, babe. You're stuck with me."

Beth Anne smiled at that. "Did you have any dinner? You must be hungry."

"I could eat a little something," he answered.

They enjoyed a little snack and comforting laughter, before going upstairs to check on the children, who were sleeping peacefully. Both looked so cute, Jennifer hugging her favorite teddy bear and Robby with his *Superman* comics, spread out all over his blanket. Leaving the kids in cozy slumber, the two then made their way to their own bedroom and dressed for bed. Rob cleaned himself up a little, then finally turned down the lights and slipped into bed.

Even though he was exhausted, it was difficult to ignore Beth Anne in her silky PJs. *She is so sexy,* Rob thought, with a smile; *she seems to look better every day. Amazing.* Beth Anne smiled back and said goodnight, as Rob hit the pillow. He was so beat, he dozed off instantly, in her warm embrace.

*

The next morning, the clock radio was blaring an irritating morning show, for what seemed like forever, before Rob could muster enough energy to get up to turn it off. He woke to an empty bed, Beth Anne already in the shower.

When she came out in her bathrobe, with her hair up in a towel, he asked her to come over and sit on the bed. He had something he needed to say to her.

"Honey, I helped to kill a man last night," he quietly said.

Beth Anne jumped off of the bed and hugged him, tightly. "Well, like we said last night: thank God *you* are okay!" she squealed. Then, she knelt, facing him.

"Thank you for telling me what happened. I know you always want to protect me, but you don't have to hide things from me, Rob."

Relieved that she had taken his confidence so well, Rob finished dressing, feeling a little less heavy. Then, he went to wake the kids, to get them ready for school. Once downstairs, he put on a fresh pot of coffee, and took out milk and cereal for the little ones.

As usual, Jennifer was the first down the stairs.

"Jen, you're always such a good girl," Rob said, "but can you please go back upstairs and get your brother up?"

"Okay, Daddy," she beamed, never one to miss out on an opportunity to boss her younger sibling around, "but you know he'll only gripe about it." She scurried back upstairs.

Rob was still putting out the cereal bowls, when he heard his son complaining and his daughter barking orders; he chuckled. Nothing seemed to be doing, though, until Beth Anne entered the scene – she may have been a gentle, loving mother, but when her kids were being insubordinate, she was worse than Rob's old drill sergeant! "Don't make me call your father up here! You two get in there and brush your teeth, comb your hair and wash up. No faking it, either! You've got fifteen minutes to finish and hightail it down those stairs for breakfast. Let's go!" she demanded.

Rob smiled. Just for today, he didn't have to be the bad guy; the one rounding them up in the morning ritual.

Breakfast went as usual – until little Robby tipped his glass over, spilling orange juice all over his new shirt.

With a sigh of exasperation, rather than anger, Beth Anne removed the sticky shirt – she didn't appear so happy when Jennifer began to laugh at her brother. "If you think it's so funny, young lady, you can go upstairs and bring me another shirt for your brother," she said, with a stern look.

"Okay, Mom," Jennifer replied with a hard-done-by frown, before taking off with her marching orders.

Rob finished his coffee and left for work a little earlier than usual, aware that he would have a lot to do after yesterday's arrest. Instead of taking the Mustang, he went into the garage and jumped into his old Chevy pickup. It burnt a little oil, but it still ran fine; it was a reliable ride for the ten-minute commute.

Outside the police station's entrance, Roy was sitting on a bench, enjoying his own cuppajo. "Rob, how you doing?" he asked.

"I'm okay, Chief. Beth Anne was a little concerned, but she calmed down after we talked it over. So, what's the deal with the case?"

"Step inside," the chief said.

He led Rob into his office, where he handed him a fresh cup of steaming-hot coffee from the percolator on his side table. "Rob, this has turned into something this little town has never seen before: a big-time drug bust. I can't believe the amount of drugs we confiscated; my god, our evidence room looks like a cartel shopping mall! The feds are in the planning room as we speak."

"The feds?"

"F.B.I., D.E.A.... you name it. They've identified our wounded prisoner as Enrico Maldez; the dead man was his cousin, Hidalgo Morales. They are Colombian; both relatives of a well-known cartel ringleader.

"As if that's not enough, those parasites from the press are all over it. I've seen reporters from New York, for God's sake! Can you believe it, Rob? The Big Apple reporting news about our little town? Even the big networks are calling and asking questions. We need to be prepared, before the questions start flying."

"Okay, I get it: the bust is big news," Rob replied. "That means you need to do the talking; I'll just be your backup and follow your lead. As far as I'm concerned, we had no choice with this Hidalgo character; we all know how it went down: it was them or us."

"That's right, Rob, and we'll just tell the truth. To be honest, my plan is to palm things off to the F.B.I.; they love this kinda stuff. We've gotta meet with them in an hour."

They finished their coffee as they went over the files, then gathered up the paperwork for the meeting.

"You ready?" the chief asked.

"As ready as I'll ever be," Rob said. "Let's go."

In the planning room, several men in expensive suits were seated around the table, along with a young, attractive woman; the state police captain and the two troopers involved in the chase were present, too. The woman – blonde, in a snappy suit – came over to Rob.

"I'm Special Agent Tracy Sanders, and this is my supervisor, Assistant Director Richard Danwick. We're with the F.B.I. Counter-Terrorism Division."

The man was tall and important-looking, with gray hair which made him look even more intimidating, and a distinguished smiled. He offered handshakes around the table, as Sanders continued:

"We have reviewed the reports and the evidence; one of our agents is questioning the prisoner as we speak. We have a few questions for the group, and we might wish to speak with some of you individually." As she spoke, she was looking directly at Rob, so intently that it almost made him want to squirm in his chair.

"Hey, Rob, I think she likes me," whispered his buddy, Detective Santo. "Wow, man, she sure is cute!"

"Not a chance, pal: she's been staring at *me* this whole time," Rob quietly teased. "Now, shut up, before you blow it for me!"

Roy handled the briefing well, and answered the inquiries in his usual confident and reassuring way. Then, questions were fielded around the table. Everyone told the same story, because it was the truth.

Afterward, Special Agent Sanders stood up. "Thank you all for your cooperation. As you know, these matters are to be kept strictly confidential. Except for Sergeant Marrino and Chief Roy, you are excused."

Santo gave Rob a jealous look as he left the room, and Rob just grinned and shrugged in response.

"Shall we go to your office, Chief?" Special Agent Sanders asked. "It might be more private."

"Sure," the chief replied, "just follow me down the hallway."

As soon as the four of them had taken a seat around the chief's desk, Sanders cut right to the chase, looking at Rob once again: "Officer Marrino, I must say that you boast a very impressive background."

"You checked me out?" Rob asked, with a crooked, uncertain smile.

"Of course," she said, matter-of-factly. "Now, as you were the first on the scene, I'd like to hear the story from your point of view."

In the gaze of her aqua-blue eyes, Rob lost his train of thought for a moment. When he could finally move his mouth again, he explained: "With all due respect, Agent Sanders, Chief Roy and the others already told you what went down. I just happened to be in the right place at the right time – a lucky break, otherwise they might have gotten away."

"And the shooting?" she blurted.

"We had no choice in the matter: when a man levels a loaded AK-47 at you, it's shoot to kill – at least, in my book."

Finally, Sanders smiled: "Well, *lucky* is right. I would say it was more that the suspects were in the *wrong* place at the *wrong* time. The truth is that we've been surveilling their operation for over a year, just waiting for an opportunity to bust the cartel. Thanks to you, Chief, and your people, their number-two man is permanently out of commission, and their main enforcer is behind bars."

Assistant Director Danwick chimed in: "We'll squeeze that one until he gives us more details; we need names and locations. Those two thugs had hundreds of pounds of clean, pure cocaine, with a street value of well over five million dollars." He sipped his coffee, allowing the number to sink in, then continued: "With your help, Chief, we have achieved a major victory in the war on drugs.

"However, I should offer you a word of caution: these people have huge power and far-reaching influence, with ties to several known terrorist cells." Rob was stunned at the developing situation, as the director continued: "I don't want anyone to feel threatened but, as a precaution, I advise tight security on this prisoner."

After another sip, he went on: "We aim to completely dismantle this drug ring, ladies and gentlemen. The deceased was Hidalgo Morales, younger brother of Juan E. Morales, the kingpin of a major Colombian cartel. It turns out the prisoner was carrying a fake I.D.; he's not the cousin – he is actually Enrico Morales, the youngest of those three badass brothers. He is also the prime suspect in a series of drug-related murders in the New York area. We plan to be very careful; we're moving him to maximum security today."

"What about those reporters?" the chief asked. "Those sharks are in a frenzy, smellin' blood in the water."

The director laughed. "No worries; Agent Sanders and I will handle most of the press inquiries. We will also meet with the D.E.A., to exchange information about the cartel. Agent Sanders, do you have anything to add?"

"Nothing much, sir, other than that we will be following this case very closely. If anyone has anything to add at any time, please give us a call." She then passed over contact information for both her and Director Danwick.

"Thank you," Chief Roy said, as they stood to leave. "We will be in touch."

As they were leaving, Agent Sanders took Rob's hand. "Please be careful, and do let us know if you need or find any more information about the case."

"Thanks," Rob replied, "I will."

After the feds had left, Chief Roy sat back down in his chair and sighed, sinking deeply. "Rob, we're gonna have to be careful here. I'm going to put extra watch on the station and put out an overtime patrol for the area, until that bad-news prisoner gets the hell outta Dodge. As for you, I want you to take the rest of the day off, with pay; lie low for a while. The F.B.I. and I will handle those bloodsucking journalists."

"Thanks, Chief," Rob said, happy to oblige.

On his way out of the station, he ran into a group of agents, escorting the prisoner to a holding area. He stopped to let them pass.

Spotting Rob, the prisoner suddenly lunged forward, with a wild look in his eyes, struggling like an animal to break free and get at him. The guards grabbed him firmly, wrestling him to the floor, as he desperately flailed and kicked, cursing in Spanish. He pointed at Rob, anger brewing in his dark eyes.

"You!" he screamed. "Yes, you are the one! You murdered my brother!"

As the man fought, everyone in the station rushed over to help the guards, struggling to put leg chains on him. Rob just watched.

"You will pay!" the Colombian shouted, as they finally managed to drag him away. "There will be a curse! You will pay!"

While some of the officers just rolled their eyes, dismissive of empty threats, Rob was visibly shaken. Something about the way Enrico had spoken his words – the evil lurking in his eyes – chilled Rob to the bone.

"Don't worry about that lunatic," Chief Roy said, as he walked Rob to his car; "he's going away for a long, long time. The only curse he's gonna have to worry about is Bubba's revenge." The chief grinned.

Rob laughed, although he had trouble finding any humor in the situation. His hands were shaking again, and he struggled to relax them.

"Just go home and get some rest," the chief said. "You deserve it."

"Thanks, Roy. I'll be okay." Then, Rob suddenly seemed to protest: "It wasn't our fault! If that dude with the AK-47 had a few more seconds, he would have killed us all!"

"I know, Rob. Without a doubt, under the circumstances, we did the right thing," Roy calmed him. "Just go home and forget about Morales. I'll call you if anything comes up."

"Thanks again for the time off," Rob said.

Roy smiled; "You've earned it, my friend. I'll see you in the morning."

On the ride home, Roy's words kept repeating, over and over, in Rob's mind: *"He's going away for a long, long time."* He really hoped it was true.

*

The next day, every newspaper and television news program was slathered with details of the story. In the official F.B.I. statement, they took most of the credit for the big bust. It was the talk of the town for weeks – until the next sensational story came along.

"The one thing you can rely on with the news is that it's fickle," Chief Roy always said. He was right about that.

It was the start of a new baseball season, and Rob busied himself by getting things ready for the team. He was excited to serve as head coach, and his neighbor Herman was going to assist; Rob was also happy to hear that one of the mothers had agreed to be the scorekeeper for the season.

While baseball took his mind off of police work for a while, he couldn't help but check the patrol reports daily, and he talked with the other officers whenever he could. Around town, he kept an eye out for anything unusual, even talking to the gossip hounds at Sammy's Bar; none of them had heard about any suspicious activity.

"There will be a curse. You will pay!"

He recalled those words time and time again, both in waking hours and in his sleep. As hard as he tried, he could not shake the ominous feeling he had. The Colombian's dark, evil eyes haunted his dreams, and he would wake up in a cold sweat. It was the same eerie feeling – that sense of impending doom – as he had experienced in the jungles of Vietnam.

Unfortunately, if there was one thing that 'Nam had taught him, it was that his instincts were usually right.

Chapter 3
EMOTIONS

Things were going well at work, especially when Rob heard he was in line for another promotion. The extra pay would be nice, and a great help in building up the college fund. The town, meanwhile, seemed as peaceful as ever.

Nevertheless, thoughts of the bust often filled his mind, especially during his commutes to and from baseball practice. But, as the weeks went by, he thought about it less and less, until eventually he found a way to put it behind him. *Life's too short,* he told himself; *it's time to move on and stop worrying about what might happen. We were only doing our job, after all.*

Whenever he returned home from ball practice, Robby rushed to help his dad unpack the gear and put it away in the garage. The little guy loved his baseball, so much so that he watched every inning of the Yankees games with his father. He had amassed an enormous collection of baseball cards, which occupied every corner and shelf in his room.

"Dinner!" they heard Beth Anne call from the kitchen.

"C'mon, son," Rob said, and the two of them hurried upstairs to clean up.

On the way, Rob found Jennifer in her room, with her

nose in a book, as usual. "Dinner's ready. What's that you're reading?"

"It's for history class, about the Civil War."

He was keen to continue the conversation, but Beth Anne yelled up the stairs:

"Rob, phone for you! It's your Army friend from Texas."

Rob smiled; he was always happy to hear from Tex, a lifelong friend he had made long ago, during his tour in Vietnam. His real name was Richard Larson, and he was one of the only people who still called Rob "Doc".

"Hey, Tex," Rob said, picking up the call in the bedroom. "How you doing?"

"Howdy, Doc. I ought to be asking you that question. What's going on up there?"

"What do you mean?" Rob said.

"I heard about that big drug bust. I've been meanin' to give you a call anyway, buddy."

"Oh, that," Rob said. He went on to fill Tex in with the details.

He was glad that his friend had kept in touch with him over the years. Tex was a tall, lanky, retired Marine sniper of legendary strength and endurance, and they were together in the thick of things, in 'Nam. They talked about old times for a while, and made plans to get the families together the coming summer.

"Well, just take care of you and yours," Tex rounded up, before they said their goodbyes.

"You do the same, Tex," Rob said with a smile, before

they hung up.

He hurried down the stairs. By the time he had finished chatting with Tex, Beth Anne had already set the table, and they were all excited to gather around the table, to enjoy a nice, hot dinner. Rob immediately dug into his meatloaf, even as Beth Anne served up the mashed potatoes and gravy.

Dinner was the family's chance to spend a little time together, and to talk about whatever was new in their lives. Jennifer was doing well in school, and proudly announced that she had made the honor list again. Rob was very proud of Jennifer; school had always been easy for her, and her grades reflected it. Beth Anne was happy to hear that Jennifer was thinking about joining the student council.

Robby had always struggled a little academically, but he was doing much better now, thanks to help from his mother and the homework club. Mostly, though, he was excited about the big ball game on Saturday.

"Shoot! I have to work," Beth Anne said, "but I'll try to get there for the second half."

After dinner, Rob helped to clear the table, then collapsed onto the couch, quickly falling asleep in front of the T.V.

Beth woke him with a kiss, sometime later. "Hey, let's go, big boy. The kids are sound asleep."

Rob watched her start for the stairs, and couldn't take his eyes off of the outline of her black panties, through the sheer nightgown she wore. He smiled; it didn't take him long to get up for the occasion.

*

On Saturday morning, Rob woke early, and quietly slipped out of bed. He didn't want to wake Beth Anne or the kids, so he grabbed his clothes and went to the downstairs bathroom to dress.

His promotion had more responsibility, so he needed to head to the station and check on a few things. By the time he walked in, everyone at the front desk was already deep in their coffee and donuts, but they had left enough for him to join them. With a steaming mug in hand, he perused the usual overnight reports, and put the finishing touches on piles of paperwork.

He worked quickly, and by noon he was on his way home, to be sure that Robby was all suited up and ready for the big game.

"I really hate that I have to work," Beth Anne said. But, she refused to leave before giving her son his weekly pep talk.

"Robby, be a good sport and have fun," she told him. "I'll try to be there before the end of the game." She then turned to Rob and gave him a goodbye kiss. "Good luck, Coach. The ice cream's on me tonight."

"Bye, Mom," Robby said, then ran over to the door to hug her.

Jennifer came down the stairs, just as her mother was

leaving. She liked to watch the games with her girlfriends, and of course she'd hit her dad up for snack bar money, before the last pitch was thrown.

Finally, Rob threw the last of the gear into the truck and off they went.

There was a good crowd at the baseball field. Rob made up the team roster, and Herman sent the boys out onto the field to warm up.

The first innings went by quickly; three up, three down. Then, as the final inning drew closer, both teams began hitting and scoring. After a few walks and a couple of hits, Robby's team was ahead by one. The head coach of the other team acted like it was the Major League, yelling and screaming at every one of his batters, terrifying the young players until they were shaking in their cleats.

*

At the end of her shift, Beth Anne was jogging through the hospital's front lobby, grabbing her keys from her purse, as she hurried to her car. She was tired, but eager to get to her son's game. She didn't notice the man who watched her as she walked past: a stranger, standing next to the trees, in the landscaped area next to the parking lot.

She noticed when he came up quickly behind her, and gasped as he tackled her to the ground.

She fought desperately, doing everything she could to stop him from placing that cloth over her mouth. "Stop!"

she screamed, kicking and squirming, and doing everything she could to break free from his powerful grasp. "Who are—" she tried to say, but before she could even finish the question, her head began to spin into oblivion, as the chemicals in the cloth overtook her.

Within seconds, another man pulled up alongside them, in a large, black van. Quickly, the two of them placed her in the back of the van and drove off.

*

At the game, Robby looked over at his dad, from his place on the bench. "Hey, Dad, is Mom here yet?"

The question caught Rob by surprise, and he darted his eyes about the bleachers. "No, son, I guess not. She must have had an emergency at work. Don't worry, though; I'm sure she'll be here any minute."

Rob put away any concern about his wife for a moment, turning his attention back to the field. His pitcher was wearing down; looking tired, and lobbing balls off-target so badly that he walked the first two batters. The team was still up by one run, but they were out of pitchers.

"Hey, Robby, you think you could throw a few?" Rob asked his son.

"I don't know, Dad," the boy said, suddenly with a serious look on his face.

"Why not?" Rob asked, with an encouraging smile. "You've got a good, strong arm and a good eye. Just try your best. And remember what Mom said: it's only a game. Our man on the mound is losing his grip a little; throwing wild ones."

"I know, Dad, but..."

"I can ask someone else if you want," Rob said. "It's your call, buddy, but we have to pull him."

Robby thought about it for just a moment longer, before his young eyes brightened. "Dad... er, Coach... put me in. I know I can do it." Then, he added: "Please? Can I? Please, can I try?"

Rob laughed and sat him down. "Okay, pal, now just relax. Throw it like we're playing catch in the back yard."

Rob caught the umpire's attention to stop the game, then walked his son to the mound.

The kid warmed up and started to throw some great pitches, straight and hard in the pocket. It was a pleasure to watch. Additionally, Rob took great delight in seeing the shock on Mr. Macho's face, as the ball snapped into the catcher's glove, again and again. After three up, two strikeouts and a pop fly to first base, the game was over.

As the team celebrated, high-fiving each other and cheering, Rob walked over to his son and gave him a big hug. "Good job, Robby."

"It was just like you said, Dad: I just pretended we were playing catch in the yard, and it worked!"

Rob smiled. "It sure did, and you were great! I am proud of you, Robby."

As the two teams lined up to shake hands, the opposing

coach called Rob aside. "Hey, Marrino, that was some lucky break we gave you," he said, with a smug grin on his face. "You know we shoulda won."

Rob's anger surged, and the muscles in his arms tightened. "You know what, pal?" he said, very softly: "I'm glad you called me over, because I've been wanting to talk to you for a long time. You, sir, are a big-ass bully, who's got no right coaching little league."

"Me? Well, you're a no-good son-of-a—"

Rob grabbed the man's elbow and pulled him away from the crowd. "Come on, now; no yelling like that in front of the kids!"

"What are you gonna do about it?" the coach demanded.

"I'm going to report your conduct to the league director. He's a close friend of a friend – if you know what I mean?"

Rob waited for a response, never taking his eyes off of the man. Mr. Macho just stood there, his mouth agape and fear brewing in his eyes. He slowly backed away, as he replied: "I've done nothing wrong. You think they'll all listen to you, just because you're a cop?"

Rob smiled. "Hmm, I don't know. Maybe I'll ask my friend to have you kicked out of the league, just to find out. These boys deserve to have a little fun out here; it's their game to win or lose – not yours." Rob didn't budge an inch.

Clearly irritated, the man finally backed off, turning to make a beeline to his wife. He angrily said something into her ear, then pointed over at Rob; she gave Rob a cold stare, before the two of them stormed off. Rob rushed over to congratulate his team.

Since Beth Anne was still at work, he had to treat the winners himself, at the concession stand. The players and their parents celebrated the victory with Italian ice and ice cream; it was a good time for everyone.

"I just wish Mom was here to see me pitch," Robby said, a little sad.

"I know, son," Rob said. "I'm sure she hated missing it."

"She never misses a game," Jennifer added; "I hope she's okay."

During the ride home, the celebrating continued. Even Jennifer praised her brother; Rob enjoyed seeing his children getting along so well. As soon as they reached the house, he was thrilled to tell his son that the game ball was his.

The little guy's eyes brightened. "Thanks, Dad! I'm gonna put it on my shelf, next to my card collection."

Rob smiled at his namesake. "Sounds like a great place for it, buddy. That was some good baseball; I want you to know that I'm very proud of you. It was great seeing your pitches zipping in there."

"Thanks, Dad."

As Rob pulled the old truck into the driveway, he noticed that Beth Anne's car was still missing.

"Where is Mom, anyway?" Jennifer asked. "She should be home by now. She never works this late."

Rob tried not to show his growing concern, as he didn't want to worry the kids. "Like I said, she probably had an emergency at the hospital. I'm sure she'll be home before we know it."

Still, as soon as he got inside, he checked the answering machine. To his surprise, there were no messages. He heated up an easy dinner for the children, then put on a pot of coffee.

Right after dinner, Jennifer went upstairs, to make a start on her homework. Before long, Rob found himself telling them to brush their teeth and head to bed.

"What about Mommy?" Jennifer asked, as he tucked his daughter in.

"I'm sure it's alright," he said, though he was becoming less and less convinced.

Heading back downstairs, he checked the time again. *Where is she?* he wondered. He finally called the hospital, hoping that she was still there.

"No, she left hours ago," said the floor nurse who answered the call. "She was really excited about going to the game."

Rob thanked her and hung up. Now he was worried. The ball field was only a few minutes away from the hospital.

Fingers of fear gripped his body and mind. It was so unlike her to go anywhere without calling, and she certainly wouldn't miss Robby's game, if she had a chance to be there. He called Beth Anne's parents, but they reported that they had not seen or heard from her, either.

Time ticked by – hour after agonizing hour – and there

was still no word.

"Where are you, honey?" Rob muttered, slowly giving in to the fear which had been quietly consuming him. It was that same ominous feeling he'd had in the jungles of Vietnam: that sensation that something was terribly, terribly wrong. The kids were already in bed, and he did not want to alarm them, but he desperately wanted to go out to look for his wife.

Clinging to a narrow thread of hope, he picked up the phone and dialed with shaking hands.

"Herman, are you awake?"

"I am now."

"Good. I need your help."

Within five minutes, Herman was at the door, and Rob quickly blurted the problem to him.

Herman smiled, initially certain that his neighbor was pulling another practical joke on him – it didn't take him long to sense that Rob wasn't fooling around.

"Look, don't worry about the kiddos," he said; "I'll stay here with them. I'll sleep on the couch 'til you get back."

"Thanks, Herman. I really need to get out there and look."

Rob then went into the kitchen and got on the phone again.

"Hello?" groaned a tired but familiar voice on the other end, after several rings.

"Chief, I'm sorry to wake you so late, but something's wrong: it's Beth Anne. I can't... She's missing, Roy! She left the hospital to meet us at the game, but never showed up. I called Bill and she's not there, either. She's left no messages and no word with anyone. Where the hell could she be at this hour?"

"Calm down, Rob," Roy replied. "I'm sure there must be a reasonable explanation for all this: maybe her car broke down on some back road. I'll call it in and tell the patrols to be on the lookout for her."

"Okay, Roy. You're right: I just need to calm down and think clearly."

"Get down to the hospital; we'll start from her last known location," the chief said.

"Okay, see ya there," Rob replied. "Thanks, Chief."

After thanking Herman once more, Rob slipped out of the door and hurried to his vehicle.

On the way to the hospital, he kept an eye out for Beth Anne. He drove down the back roads slowly, looking around every corner, but there was no sign of her or her car. When he pulled into the hospital parking lot, the chief was already waiting for him there.

"Roy, I-I don't know where the hell she is! It's not like her at all, to miss the game and go somewhere without calling. She can't have just disappeared."

"I know," the chief said.

"Oh, my god; you don't think... she would just leave us... would she? If she has, I don't understand why; it doesn't make any sense."

"Rob, she's a good mom; she wouldn't have missed the

game if she could have helped it. I've got all eyes on it; we'll find her. For now, let's keep our cool and think clearly. If she had an accident or broke down... well, then I'm sure one of our patrols will pick her up any minute."

Rob and Roy walked around the back of the hospital parking lot, looking for her car. The place was almost deserted at that hour; it wasn't long before they found it.

Rob opened the door with his key, then revved the engine with no problems. "It's running okay. Why'd she leave it here?" he asked, the panic growing inside him.

"I don't know, Rob," the chief said. "We'll figure it out. C'mon."

Rob's hands started to tremble, as they made their way around the perimeter of the hospital – no Beth Anne; there was no sign of her inside, either. He called home to check with Herman, who hadn't seen or heard from her; her parents could tell him nothing, either. It was getting very late now.

"I'll call in an official missing-persons report," the chief said, with a sigh. "We'll put out an A.P.B. for her."

Knowing they had no time to waste, they did their best to come up with a plan: Rob and the night shift would stay out on patrol and keep searching; if there was no sign of her by morning, Rob would stop by the house to pick up the kids, and drop them off to stay with their grandparents, Bill and Susan.

All through the night, Rob drove, searching every nook and cranny of town. He questioned everyone he met, in any shops which were still open and on the streets, but no one had any information.

He started to think about the Colombian, and those threatening, hateful words he had spewed. But, he was quick to put that out of his mind; the very thought terrified him.

Calm down, he told himself; *stay positive.*

Several hours later, now out of options, he headed over to his in-laws' house, hoping and praying that her parents had received some word. When he arrived, the worried, forlorn looks on their faces was the only answer he needed – albeit not the answer he wanted, or was praying to hear.

"I just don't understand it," Susan said, filling their coffee cups, after Rob had filled them in with what little he knew.

"Me, either," Rob said. "She was supposed to meet us at the game. According to the floor nurse, she left the hospital a little after six – but her car is still parked there, and it's running fine. She works less than ten minutes from the game, which ended at seven; even if she had walked, she would have still had plenty of time to get there."

"So, what now?" Bill asked.

"Well, Roy has issued an A.P.B. Everyone is searching for her."

Susan started sobbing. "My Beth Anne! Pray for our little girl. She means everything to us!"

After coffee, Bill walked Rob to his car, where he too broke down in tears, as he grabbed Rob's hand. "Please, Rob, please find out what the hell has happened to her!"

Rob looked sincerely at his broken-hearted father-in-law. "The kids will be here in the morning, if that's okay with you."

"Of course," Bill said, with a sniffle.

"Bill, I will find her – even if I have to go to the ends of the Earth. You will see your daughter again."

"I hope so, Rob; I really hope so."

After the visit, Rob was feeling tired and worn out. His nerves were on edge, as he ran to his car and grabbed the radio. Dispatch had received no word. So, he just hopped in... and drove, and drove, and drove some more, examining every roadside, street and alley.

Eventually, he reached his church. He got out of his car, sat on the steps and prayed, as his tears came in torrents – tears he was no longer able to hold back. His love for her was so strong, but the anger he was starting to feel nearly tore him in two.

She would never leave us! he silently fumed. *Never by choice. So, what happened to her? Was it them? Was it those drug-smuggling terrorists? But, how? One is dead; the other is behind bars.*

Approaching footsteps jolted Rob from his thoughts; he turned to see Father Peter, holding out a hand and smiling at him.

"Please, my son, come inside; I think you need to talk. You've been out here for some time."

Rob sobbed and nodded, following the clergyman into the dimly-lit church. They sat on a pew near the altar.

Father Peter said a short prayer, then asked, in his calm, reassuring voice:

"What brings you to the Lord's house so late at night, to sit alone and cry? Perhaps I can help you in some way."

Rob took a moment to gather his thoughts, thankful that there was something calming about being in the church. He revealed his fears and concerns, and they prayed together – the prayers filled Rob with renewed hope. Afterward, he thanked Father Peter, and left feeling calmer and more clear-headed.

He called the station again, to learn that there had still been no word or sign of her anywhere. He had never felt so drained or depressed. He wanted to go home and check on the kids. *Later,* he thought to himself; *I need to see Roy and make arrangements with him. I need to keep searching for Beth Anne.*

Arriving at home, Rob walked into the kitchen, found his bottle of aged bourbon and poured himself a drink. Then, he sat down on the couch next to his friend.

"The kids are sound asleep," Herman said. "How are things going?"

Rob took a long pull from his drink. "Nothing is going – nothing at all. That's the problem, Herman: we've got nothing to go on – except that she's gone. Chief Roy has put out a statewide A.P.B."

"Well, let me know," Herman said, clapping Rob on the shoulder as he stood up. "Call me if there's anything I can do to help."

"Thanks, Herman; you're a good friend. I've got a gut feeling, but... well, I just don't want to believe it yet. I'm tired, and my nerves are shot, but I'll find her, somehow. Then, this nightmare will be over."

Herman finished his soda in one gulp. "If anyone can find her, it's you," he said. "Just try to get some rest when you can."

After Herman had left, Rob checked the answering machine, but to no avail. Upstairs, he peeked in on his children, and found them sound asleep. He had no idea how he was going to break the awful news to them; he knew that he needed to be as delicate as possible. He poured himself another strong one, then stretched out on the couch.

Now and then, he dozed off, but his mind was full of thoughts of Beth Anne. He wondered where she was, and what she was going through. His instincts and his experience told him increasingly that this had something to do with the drug bust, but he did not want to give in to his worst fears; he chose, instead, to cling to the hope in his heart.

A few hours later, Rob woke with a start, to the sound of the ringing phone. He ran to answer it, praying he would hear his wife's voice on the other end.

"Anything?" Bill asked, sniffling into the receiver.

Rob sighed, in frustration and fear. "No, nothing," he said.

"Well, I was hoping you'd have some good news. I'll see

you when you bring the kids over this morning."

Rob called Roy, and they agreed to meet later at the station. Rob started trying to get on with the day, as best he could.

"Why can't this all just be a bad dream?" he muttered aloud to himself, as he put the coffee on and poured the kids' orange juice, getting things ready for their breakfast. As he was walking upstairs to get them up for school, he decided that it would be best to tell them she was still tied up at the hospital.

After a quick shower and change of clothes, Rob found the kids already downstairs at the breakfast table. He told them their mom was working.

Robby accepted the excuse with a shrug, but Jennifer seemed more concerned. "Can I go to the hospital to see her, after school?"

"Uh, I'm not sure that's a good idea, honey. Your mom is working, and there are so many... uh... germs... there; we don't want you getting sick. In fact, I think you two should spend some time at Grandma's house for a while, 'til things settle down for your mom."

"Okay, Dad," Jennifer added. "Just tell Mom to call us at Grandma's."

"Sure thing, honey," Rob replied. "Now, let's get your things ready."

*

Beth Anne's mother was sitting on the porch when Rob pulled into the driveway. She gave her grandchildren a huge hug, then sent them inside to put their things away.

"Rob," she said, looking at him from her wooden rocker, "you look so tired. Come inside; I'll make you some bacon and eggs."

Rob hugged her. "Susan, I just appreciate you taking care of Jennifer and Robby. I have to find her. I *will* find her," he promised, once again.

Her voice trembled, as she said: "Rob, you know the kids will be fine here; don't worry about them. Please, just find our Beth Anne. You have my faith, my hope and my prayers. You're going to need energy, too, though, so come on in and have some breakfast before you go."

Rob reluctantly walked inside, desperately trying to think of some way to explain the situation to his children – to be more truthful, without upsetting them too much. He continued gathering his thoughts, as everyone sat down at the table.

Finally, he managed to start: "You two need to stay with Grandma and Grandpa, 'til I get back."

"Where you goin', Dad?" Robby asked, his mouth full of bacon.

"I've got to go help your mom."

"At the hospital?" Jennifer asked, confused.

"No, honey; she's... lost somewhere, and she needs me to help her get back home."

Jennifer quietened, and her eyes grew wide.

Rob leaned toward his daughter. "Honey, it's going to be okay."

She jumped up out of her seat and hugged Rob, tightly. "Daddy, what is up with Mom? I thought you said she was at the hospital; now, you're saying she's lost! Where is she? Is she okay?"

Rob held his trembling daughter in his arms, fighting back tears of his own. "Jennifer, you have to promise me to be strong and to take care of your brother. I promise you, I will bring your mom home; she will be here real soon."

She kissed him gently on the cheek. "Okay, Dad: I promise to be strong. I know you'll find her and bring her back to us."

After finishing his plate and saying his goodbyes, Rob headed for the door.

"Hold on, son," Bill said; "I'll walk you out."

When they reached Rob's car, Bill told him: "Rob, go home and get some rest; I'll pray that you find her alive and well. If you need anything, please let me know."

"Thanks, Bill," Rob said, taking hold of the man's hand. "I do need some more sleep, to clear my head. I'll keep you and Susan informed; like Father Peter said, we need to pray and find strength in our love for her. Oh, I almost forgot: he might stop by later, to talk with Susan and the kids."

"That's good; he's always welcome here," Bill said.

As Rob drove home, he was tired to the bone, but at least he had a full stomach. Most importantly, he still had hope.

He could hardly keep his eyes open, but on arriving

home he checked the answering machine once more. There were no new messages, so he trudged up the stairs and undressed. He passed out the moment his head hit the pillow.

*

Over 150 miles away, a black van pulled off of the interstate, onto a long, winding, gravel road, which led to a remote field – a long, wide and flat stretch, which made a perfect landing strip. Once the van had come to a stop, Beth Anne's abductors drank beer and ate sandwiches, while they waited for the plane.

Beth Anne was in the back, lying on the floor with duct tape over her mouth; her feet and hands were tied and bound. She kept drifting in and out of consciousness, the drugs still coursing through her system.

Before long, a small plane landed on the isolated, makeshift runway, and the men quickly and efficiently put Beth Anne on board. As they did, another man jumped out of the plane, holding a large holdall full of drugs. He quickly took off in the van.

The little plane accelerated, and lifted off of the dirt and gravel runway. Once it had gained altitude, it turned southward.

*

Rob woke slowly to the beeping of his alarm clock. He had only managed four hours of sleep, but that would have to do. He jumped into the shower, and within half an hour was on his way out again. Time was of the essence; he had to do something before the trail got cold. Before he left, he called in, hoping that there was some word on Beth Anne, but no one had spotted her.

On the way to the station, Rob stopped by the hospital, to have another look around. He drove slowly around the parking lot, before parking next to his wife's abandoned car.

Officer Santo, the night watchman, walked over to Rob's car. "Rob, if I can do anything at all, you know I'm here for you. I've gotta head home for some shuteye, but don't hesitate to call if you need me."

"Thanks, Santo; I may take you up on that. For now, I just want to have another look around the place."

Rob felt a little better after talking to Santo for a few minutes, but he had work to do. He walked to the hospital's main entrance, then turned around, attempting to retrace the steps she would have taken back to her car. As he approached her vehicle, he noticed a small, landscaped area ahead, with the trace of a path worn through it – clearly a shortcut. He wondered if she might have gone that way, rather than the sidewalk, to save time.

Moving slowly, and using his flashlight to peer into any shadows, he walked back and forth along the path.

Then, on his third pass, he saw something glinting. At first, he thought it was the flashlight's beam reflecting off of a discarded beer bottle – but, when he moved closer, he saw that it was something else; he put on his gloves and bent down to pick it up. His heart sank, as he found himself holding his wife's keyring.

He circled the path again and again, until he found something else: her shattered sunglasses, lying in the grass.

His mind was a blur; for a long moment, he just sat there, trembling and unable to move. Then, in a panic, he ran to his car, stuffed everything into an envelope, and slammed the Mustang into gear.

Santo was just pulling out, when he saw the smoking tires of Rob's Mustang. He tried to stop him, yelling out of the window: "Rob! Wait! Rob, what is it? What's wrong?"

Rob ignored him and drove off like a maniac, ignoring the speed limits as he hurried to the station.

When he saw Roy waiting for him at the front desk, he ran over and dumped the contents of the envelope in front of him.

"Someone took her, Chief! I need to talk to that prisoner – the one we busted. I know those cartel terrorists had something to do with this! That devil's gonna talk, or I'll kill him, too!"

Roy was shocked and suddenly pale, as he looked down at the keys and the broken shades. "Where did you find them?"

"At the hospital; there's a little path which leads to the parking lot. Beth Anne must have taken a shortcut to her car."

Roy carefully placed the items back into the envelope. "We'll run all of this for prints. Try to calm down, Rob; we will get to the bottom of this. The F.B.I. is waiting in my office right now. I'll send a patrol over to search and secure the area by Beth Anne's car."

Rob tried his best to calm down, but he was overcome with a burning anger and a deep desire to see his wife again. "Thanks, Roy," he said. "It's just... Those bastards are unbelievable! They're gonna pay for this; it's my life for her!"

Agent Sanders was already in the chief's office, along with three other agents. She sat across from Rob and took the envelope from him, as he told her:

"I just found these – her things – along the path leading to the hospital parking lot. Now I know someone has her! Is this a bad dream, or is this really happening to me?"

Roy walked over and put his hands on Rob's shoulders. "Rob, please settle down and let Agent Sanders explain."

She came around and pulled a chair up next to Rob. "Officer Marrino, what I am about to say must not leave this room."

"Just say it," Rob said. "I want to know what happened to my wife... and why."

"As you suspect, Beth Anne *has* been taken hostage. We know our culprits are a Colombian cartel and their rebels: they have... made demands."

"What kind of demands? However much they want, I'll pay it!" Rob said, pounding a fist on the table.

"They don't want money; they demand the immediate release of the prisoner, or they claim they will take your wife's life."

Rob was speechless. He became angrier than he had ever been in his life. His hands shook, and his whole body soon followed suit.

There is no other way, he slowly realized: *I have to find her myself, or I'll lose her forever.*

Sanders continued: "We are doing everything possible to buy time – even working with the Colombian government, to get a fix on her location. This is a very difficult situation; our government does not make deals with terrorists."

Still, Rob remained silent, staring at her with a blank look on his face. He was unable to respond, as the horror of it fully consumed him.

Then, without warning, he jumped to his feet and slammed his fist on the table again. "They don't know what they have done!" he yelled. "If they harm one hair on her head, I will kill them all! My life for her! Somehow, they will pay!"

Chief Roy walked over to Rob and tried to pull him aside. "I know you're upset, Rob – that's understandable; I'm scared, too – but you have to calm down; we have to focus here. Maybe you should go home – be with your kids. We'll call if anything comes up."

Rob shook his head, reclaimed his seat, then looked around the table, wiping the sweat off of his forehead. "I don't want to go home!" he suddenly yelled, punching the table again. "I want to find my wife. What I need are details: where the hell is this cartel; who are they; where are they keeping her?"

"Rob, everything possible is being done, and everyone is looking. Maybe you should—"

"Don't tell me what I should do, Chief!" Rob interrupted. "That's my wife out there; the mother of my children!"

"And, my niece."

Agent Sanders stood up and calmly handed Rob a card. "Call me anytime, if you hear anything at all; I will contact you immediately if we discover anything. Our prayers are with you and the children, and I promise we'll get more information. But, for now, the chief is right: you should go home and be with your family."

Rob grabbed a napkin and wiped his sweating face. He did his best to regain his composure, before looking around the room again. He noticed that his hands were trembling, but he didn't care. He finally realized that he had no choice.

"Fine, I'll go. But, you'd better call me if you hear anything."

"Consider it done," Agent Sanders said.

Roy walked Rob to his car. "Take care of yourself, Rob. You'll be on paid leave, and it might be a good idea to see your doctor while you're out; maybe he can give you something to help calm you down a little."

"Thanks, Roy," Rob said; "I guess I could use something for my nerves."

"It's entirely understandable," the chief said. "Just know

that we will find her. We will!"

"I know," Rob said. More than anything, he wanted to believe it.

On the ride home, Rob thought about anything that he could possibly do, other than sitting around, waiting and taking nerve pills.

Suddenly, a thought struck him.

Tex!

Yeah, Tex. He'll know how we get to these criminals.

At that point, anything at all was worth a try – even if he had to go after them himself, with the help of his old Army buddy.

Chapter 4
PLANS

Rob called Tex as soon as he got home. There was no answer.

"Doc here, Fox Four. Copy, Fox Four?" he spoke into the answering machine; "Fox 4" was their emergency call sign in the Vietnam War. All he could do then was wait.

While he waited impatiently by the phone, he did a little research on Colombia and the known cartels. After an hour passed, Rob's frustration started to set in. *Why hasn't he called?* he wondered. He tried to comfort himself with logic: *Maybe he's away from the ranch, or out riding his horses.* Still, more anger brewed inside him with every passing minute; he couldn't stop thinking about that prisoner with the mean, black eyes.

Finally, with no return call from Tex, and fears that he would never see Beth Anne again still torturing his mind, Rob sighed and left for his doctor's appointment.

*

Meanwhile, just off the northern coast of Colombia, a small plane flew inland a few miles, before landing on the narrow, dusty runway at the cartel's base.

As the effects of the drugs wore off, Beth Anne started to become keenly aware of her surroundings, much to her dismay. She was horrified when one of the terrorists suddenly grabbed her by the arm, put a black hood over her head and led her off of the plane. She could feel the hot, moist air, as she was placed in the back seat of a vehicle.

Under the hood, she struggled to breathe. She could hear voices, talking in Spanish. Every once in a while, the men would share a laugh, as the Jeep bumped along the trail to the lockup.

Where am I, she wondered. *How will anyone ever find me in this godforsaken place?*

She feared she would never see Rob or her children again.

*

Back at F.B.I. headquarters, Agent Sanders was sat at her desk, feeling helpless, the raw emotion of the meeting with Rob still fresh in her mind. She wanted to do something productive – preferably, to bring Beth Anne back home – but she felt as if her hands were tied.

She remembered the desperation in Rob's eyes when he had demanded the details: *"Where is this cartel? Who are they? Where are they keeping her?"* She had a feeling she knew the answers to some of those questions, and she desperately wanted to do something for the poor man.

Unable to sit idly by any longer, Agent Sanders got up

and peeked out of the door, stepping into the hallway, as she looked left and right. When she was confident no one else was around, she slipped into the file room.

She quickly found what she was looking for, then hurried back to her office, manila folder in hand. She ran off some copies, ignoring the huge word *"CONFIDENTIAL"*, rubber-stamped in red on the front of the file, and each individual document.

*

In Pikesville, Rob was awaking from a drunken slumber. He was soaked with sweat, and his head felt as if he'd been pounding it into a brick wall; his nightmare seemed so real that his heart was still pounding from it, as he wiped the sweat from his face. Over the years, he had often dreamt about the war, but none of his night terrors had ever been as vivid as this one. The names and faces; all the blood; the bullets and the bandages – it was all so very real, as if he had somehow been transported back to those hot, steamy jungles again.

A little aspirin with his black coffee worked wonders, and he hoped that the nerve pill the doctor had prescribed would make him feel even better. After a quick shower, he looked down at his hands and realized that they were still shaking, as he dressed himself. His nerves were in bad shape, but at least he had got a few hours' sleep. He popped another pill.

But, no pill could alleviate that bad feeling he had, of impending danger; that foreboding sense of doom. Once again, he would have to go out into the jungles and search for the enemy.

When Rob's phone rang, he scrambled over to pick it up. "Rob here," he said quickly, his voice gruff and tired.

"What's up, Doc? Sorry I didn't call back sooner; I was out with my horses."

"Tex! Thank God you called," Rob said, relieved to finally hear from his old friend. He got straight to business: "It's Beth Anne, she's... uh... she's gone missing. I've got a gut feeling she's on her way to Colombia – if she's not there already."

"Colombia?! What the hell happened to her?"

"Those cartel terrorists took her. When I get my hands on those monsters, I'll kill them!"

"Jesus, Rob! How the hell did they find her?"

Rob took a deep breath, then filled Tex in on what had transpired, leading to the horrible situation they were now in. After he had finished talking, Tex gladly offered his help, without Rob even having had to ask.

It's good to have a friend like Tex, Rob thought, *especially in times like now.*

The two had maintained a long friendship; the previous fall, they had spent a fun-filled week together in Orlando, with their families. Tex had promised Beth Anne and the kids that they could come to his ranch and learn how to ride horses.

"I'll be on my way to New Jersey first thing in the morning," Tex promised. "I'll check with my contacts – see if anybody's got a handle on this cartel – and I'll try to come up with a game plan on the way."

"Great," Rob said. "In the meantime, I'm going to check at the station and keep looking around town for any new information. Thanks, Tex."

"No thanks are necessary, my friend; as far as I'm concerned, y'all are family. Don't worry; we'll get 'er back."

Just as Rob was heading out of the door, the phone rang again. Sure that it was Tex, calling back to mention something he had forgotten, he snatched it up. "Yeah?"

"Officer Marrino?" asked a familiar female voice.

"Yes, it's me," Rob answered. "This is Agent Sanders, right?"

"Right," she replied. "I need to see you. Can you meet me at the steakhouse tonight, at eight?"

Rob could hear from her voice that she had news – and she was not about to release any of it over the phone. Rob had got a good feeling about meeting her, and there was no way he was going to turn down her invitation. "Okay, Sanders; I'll see you then."

"Good. See you at eight," Sanders replied, and clicked off.

On his way to the station, Rob's mind raced over what to do next.

How are we gonna get out of this mess? he asked himself, again and again. But, most importantly: *How am I going to get my Beth Anne out of this alive?*

Rob arrived at the station, where he talked with Santo and some of the guys – all good friends – before Roy waved him into his office.

"You look a little better, Rob," the chief said, as he plopped down in his big leather chair. "How are the kids doing?"

"As well as can be expected," Rob said.

"Good. Rob, we managed to get a statement from one of the nurses at the hospital. She said she heard some commotion by the parking area - car doors slamming and some screaming – but, she didn't see anything. She dismissed it; thought it was just kids fooling around."

"Anything else?" Rob asked.

"Well, the feds sent police units to check airports, bus and train terminals, but we've got nothin' so far."

This time, Rob remained silent, staring at his feet. He was fully focused on what Agent Sanders might have to tell him.

"You got something on your mind?" Chief Roy said.

Snapping out of it, Rob looked up at his chief and said: "Roy, if the offer still stands, I think I am gonna take you up on that leave of absence. I need some time – a week or two – to sort things out; I think it's best that I'm home, with my kids."

Roy smiled. "Good thinking, Rob. Take as much time as you need; I'll handle things here. Did you go see the doctor?"

"I did. I think the meds are helping a little."

"Good. Don't worry about finances; if nothing else, you've got paid vacation time coming. Just don't go getting any stupid ideas; let the F.B.I. do their jobs."

Rob smiled, thanked his friend, then left the police station, to pay a visit to his in-laws and his children.

On the way, he drove past his empty house, wondering if things would ever be the same again.

*

Bill was in the living room, watching T.V., and Jennifer and Robby were busy with their homework. As soon as the little ones saw him, they dropped their pencils and books, and hurried over to their father.

"Daddy, is Mommy coming home soon?" Robby asked.

"Yeah, Dad, where is she? Did you find her?" Jennifer asked, peeking behind him with a questioning look.

"She'll be here soon," Rob said. "In fact, I'm leaving in a while to go pick her up."

Jennifer crossed her arms, stomped her foot, and took on a defiant expression which she rarely showed to her parents. "If you're going to get Mom, I'm going with you," she said.

Rob smiled and took her hand. "Honey, I have to go alone, but I promise that Mom and I will both be back. Go on and do your homework now – you don't want Mom yelling at you, do you?"

Jennifer looked at him dubiously, for a moment, then

followed her brother back to their textbooks and worksheets.

Bill got up out of his recliner and pulled Rob aside. "How are things really going, son? Any news?"

"Nothing much yet, but I may have to leave town for a few days."

"No problem, Rob. You do what you think is right; don't worry about the children."

Rob thanked his father-in-law, then walked back into the living room, where he quietly took another of his pills. Then, he stretched out on the couch, to try to relax. The kids continued with their homework, until Susan brought them some milk and freshly-baked chocolate-chip cookies. As they nibbled on their treats and watched cartoons, Rob drifted off to sleep, with the theme tune from *The Flintstones* for his lullaby.

*

When Rob awoke, he immediately checked his watch. When he realized it was six-thirty already, he was instantly awake. He bid his family farewell, then hurried out of the door, so he could go home and clean up, before his important meeting at the steakhouse.

As Rob was pulling into his driveway, a tow truck was just pulling out. While he wished his wife was at home, it was a nice feeling to see her car again parked in front of the house, where it belonged. He hoped and prayed that she would be reunited with it soon.

Feeling much better after the nap and his shower, Rob donned some fresh clothes, then left for the steakhouse.

When he arrived at the crowded restaurant, he asked for a private corner table for two. He ordered wine with appetizers, since he was a little early, and more than a little hungry.

Agent Sanders arrived right on time, just as the waiter was delivering the appetizers and a tasty bottle of red. She was wearing snug, black dress pants, a matching blouse and a short, bright-blue jacket. Her blue eyes were piercing as she came closer, capturing the gaze of every man in the room.

"Agent Sanders," Rob said, politely standing while she took her seat. "I hope you like red wine."

"Thanks, Rob; that will be fine. And it's just Tracy when we're off duty, okay?"

Rob filled her glass and smiled, sheepishly. "Okay... Tracy. Please, try the stuffed clams; they're very good."

She sipped her wine. "So, how are you and your children holding up, in the midst of all this?"

"To be honest, Tracy, I don't care about me; the kids and Beth Anne are my only concern. They're staying with their grandparents, but they keep asking for their mom – and I'm tired of lying to them. They need her as much as I do. It hurts to see the worried look in their eyes. I try not to think of what those terrorists might do to her, but it's driving me crazy; I'm worried sick, afraid that we'll never find her, or that when we do, she won't be..."

He trailed off, unable to face the potential reality. His hands began to tremble again, forcing him to put his wine glass down. He quickly picked it back up again, and took a long swig. "I pray for her, and for the strength to get me through this nightmare. I will not stop looking until we find her. I can't stop thinking about her."

Sanders gently took Rob's hand in her own. "I hope you find her, too," she said.

"Listen, Tracy, I'm sorry I sort of blew up at that meeting. I'm just so damn angry! I guess it did me good to get it out."

"Rob, are you alright... really?" she asked, looking down at his shaking hands. "Have you been getting enough sleep?"

"Not much," he admitted, trying to remain calm. "I'm not really okay – but I will be when we find her."

He took another sip of wine, then decided to cut right to it: "Tracy, I have to ask, what is the real reason for this meeting? You said you have some news – I hope it's good."

She pulled an envelope from her purse. "I'm not supposed to give you this information: it's confidential. But, you and I both know that official deals with terrorists are off the table. I wanted to do something more, so I dug into the intel on the cartel for you."

"You did?" Rob took the envelope and opened the clasp.

"Yes. I hope you don't mind, but I researched your military background – and, between you and me, I've got a gut feeling you're going to do everything in your power to get her out, with or without our help. To do that, then, you should know what we know."

"I—" Rob started, but she quickly continued:

"It would be better for us both if you keep this to yourself, though."

Caught in her gorgeous gaze, Rob hesitated for a moment. He felt some sort of intimate connection – and that brought about no small measure of guilt. Still, he finally managed to say: "Thanks, Tracy. I will go and I will find her – or I'll die trying."

"Go where? When?"

"Colombia, within a few days. I hope you can buy me some time; that your people can keep the cartel hanging for as long as possible."

"We will do whatever we can to stall them, Rob, but you're right: there isn't much time."

The sizzling steaks arrived, accompanied by a basket of fresh bread. The waiter kindly filled their wine glasses, once again.

"Excellent, huh?" Rob said, feeling much better after a good meal.

"Delicious," she said, reaching for the check with a beautiful smile on her face. "Now, take care, Doc."

He laughed; "Ah, you *have* been doing your homework, haven't you?! No one calls me 'Doc' now – other than my buddy, Tex. Thanks for dinner... and, thanks for being a friend; I know you're sticking your neck out on this one."

She stood up, but before she walked away from the table, she looked at him seriously, once more; "This conversation never happened. I will call you when I have some news."

After she left, Rob hurried to his car and opened the envelope. In it, he found a detailed map of the Bogotá area and the northern Colombian coastline, as well as several insightful documents.

Finally, he had a solid lead! But, he knew the trip and rescue mission would require a lot of careful planning. "It's now or never," he told himself as he stuffed everything back into the envelope. "Time for action."

He pulled into his driveway and parked next to Beth Anne's car, which she loved so much. He downed two pills before bed, then stared at the maps, practically memorizing every inch of them, before he finally dozed off.

*

Rob awoke early the next morning and made a quick breakfast, followed by a few quick calls, before he took off on the long drive to the airport.

As he drove along the interstate, he found himself wondering, once more: *Will I ever see her again?* He did his best to put that macabre thought out of his mind, but it was always there, teasing and torturing him; breaking his heart. He hoped to make the terrorists pay dearly for that.

Rob arrived at the busy airport center, left his car in short-term parking, then went indoors and maneuvered through the complex of terminals. He glanced at the flight number he had jotted down, then up at the information board to determine Tex's arrival, finding his way to the proper gate.

When the plane arrived, Tex wasn't too difficult to spot: the man was *big*, with long hair and a black mustache; he wore pointed-toe cowboy boots and a Stetson.

"Howdy, partner," Tex said, grabbing Rob's hand for a healthy shake. "Woulda been nice to see you under better circumstances, but it's good to see you anyway."

"Hey, Tex, good to see you, my friend," Rob said, somewhat somberly.

"Don't worry, Doc: this thing'll be all said and done before you know it. I gotta get back to my horses; there's a big auction and rodeo coming up." Tex had a big grin on his face, as he did his best to cheer up his friend.

Rob was glad to see his old pal again. "Tex," he said, shaking the cowboy's big, rough hand, "thanks for coming up right away. You're right that we gotta put a quick end to this: we don't have much time. I'll pay you for your help."

Tex grimaced. "Doc! You know I'll never forget 'Nam, and what you did for me and them other boys over there. I owe you this one, buddy. Besides, I know you'd do the same for me."

On the drive back to Rob's place, they talked about old times. Even in Vietnam, they had managed to make some good memories – and, even in Rob's distress, those memories managed to draw a smile or two out of him.

Tex lit up a Marlboro. "Like I told ya on the phone, I've still got some inside connections, Doc. I take some side jobs occasionally; I get the calls from my contact in the military, and I take a little trip – it's usually some dude who's considered a national threat. But, if you ask those government types, they'll make out they don't know I exist. It makes for a nice chunk of money here and there... It's not *just* for the money, though."

"That's good," Rob said. "I'm proud of you."

"Doc, I gotta be straight with you: it don't look good. Those cartel dudes are nasty little buggers. To make matters worse, they're in bed with and protected by F.A.R.C. – the Revolutionary Armed Forces of Colombia – which means they're well-trained and well-armed. Our country supports the Colombian government in their war against these terrorists, but in some ways it's a never-ending cycle."

Rob pulled off of the interstate and started up the mountain road in silence, mulling over the harsh reality.

Tex continued: "I did check the weather down there; the daytime high is up near a hundred, with ninety percent humidity. You ready for a 'Nam rematch, Doc? 'Cos that's just what we might be walkin' into – especially if F.A.R.C. is involved."

"Tex, at this point I don't care who's involved," Rob replied, sternly; "I'll gladly go to Hell and back again. You can opt out, though; just set me up and get back to your ranch, if you need to. It's *my* life for her, not yours."

Tex was uncharacteristically quiet for a moment, and just looking at his friend. "Thanks for giving me the choice, Doc. But, the way I see it, I wouldn't be alive if not for you;

it's all or none. So, let's giddy-up."

At the house, Rob put on some coffee and made them some sandwiches. Then, after lunch, he handed the envelope of confidential information over to Tex.

Sitting at the kitchen table, drinking coffee and smoking another Marlboro, Tex smiled as he flipped through the documents and maps. "Where'd you get this, Doc? This is top-secret stuff – much better than the info I got! It even defines F.A.R.C. as a military Marxist-Leninist organization, and mentions their possible involvement in the drugs. These details will save us a lot of time."

"Yeah, I hope so," Rob said.

Tex spread out a large, detailed map of Colombia. "Okay, so I think this should be our game plan for now: we take a flight to Bogotá, where my reliable contact will pick us up and take us northwest – along the coast – to catch our boat ride... right here..." He pointed out the position. "Then, we'll travel to a remote location, where we can pick up some gear; there, we'll sit tight and wait. We'll head inland by chopper, under the cover of night, and drop off a few klicks from the location. Then, we get into position and check out the scenery."

"Sounds good. What then?" Rob asked.

After another sip of coffee, Tex went on: "Then, we watch and learn all day, and make our move late that night. I'll take my night-vision special, and I think I might have an old Mini-16 lying around for you. For a sidearm, we'll use a pair of HK-45s, with custom silencers. Throw in a couple of my special satchel charges and some claymores, and we're on our way."

"Nice," Rob said, grinning at the thought.

Tex handed the envelope back to Rob. "Let me call my contacts and make the final arrangements; with my government clearance, I can ship the gear down there express. If all goes well, we'll snatch Beth Anne outta there and boogie on down the road; our man in the chopper will be waiting for my transponder signal, then we'll all catch our ride home."

"I love it when a plan comes together," Rob said, still smiling, with hope and a cautious feeling of relief in his heart.

"It *can* be done, partner! Speed, stealth and surprise are the only way to make it happen. Just understand though, Doc, that there's always a chance it could all go to Hell in a handbasket. If that happens, we just gotta run like hell for the transponder."

Rob jumped up, more excited than he'd felt since the whole trauma had begun. "So, when do we go?"

Tex smiled. "Soon. But, there is one thing."

"What?"

"Doc, my man and his people, the shipping on the gear and the chopper don't come cheap; I figure we'll need thirty grand."

"Whoa!" Rob said, shocked. "I was thinking maybe ten or fifteen. I'm not sure I can come up with that much cash."

"Remember, Doc, anyone who helps us is putting himself

– or herself – at risk; the price doubled the instant I mentioned the cartel. I can help out a little, if need be, but I've gotta take today off; I'll make the rest of the arrangements from the ranch. Do what you can to round up as much money as possible, then take the next flight to Texas. From there, we can be in Colombia in under twenty-four hours."

"Okay, Tex," Rob said; "I'll beg, borrow or steal if I have to."

*

They were pulling out of the driveway, for the drive back to the airport, when a car pulled up to a halt, in front of the Mustang. A striking woman stepped out and walked over to Rob's car, with a smile on her face.

"Hello, Doc. I see you've found your old friend, Tex. Are you boys going on a little trip?"

They both looked at each other and smiled, then returned their eyes innocently to Special Agent Sanders.

"We just got word," she said: "we have five days to deliver the prisoner, or else. Good luck and good hunting, fellas; you have my prayers for a happy ending. Oh, and we never had this conversation, by the way."

With that said, she walked back to her car. They could see the slight smile playing on her face, as she turned the car around and drove away.

"Five days," Rob replied. "That oughta give us enough

time."

Tex was nodding in agreement, but he couldn't seem able to pull his eyes away from Tracy Sanders. "Who in the hell was that fine-lookin' filly?"

Rob smiled. "Take a picture; it'll last longer."

Tex laughed, then asked seriously: "Can we trust her, Doc?"

"You'd better start to, Tex," Rob said, still grinning; "she's the one who gave me the envelope. She's a fine woman – and she has been a good friend."

"Well, you'd better keep away from that sweet thing," Tex smirked; "seems she's got the hots for you."

"I'm a married man, Tex," Rob said, then suddenly winced, as he thought of his Beth Anne.

"Let's hurry to the airport; I wanna get home before midnight, so we can get this show on the road."

Rob popped his police light on the roof and pulled out, into the road. "We've got three hours before rush hour; I'll have you there in no time." With that, he pinned them back in their seats, throttling the Mustang through its gears.

As promised, they made excellent time on the relatively empty interstate. Within a few hours, Rob had dropped Tex off at the terminal, and was well on his way back home.

As soon as he got home, he busied himself packing for the trip, then checked his bank accounts. While gathering the money he needed wouldn't be the easiest thing in the world, Rob already felt a little better knowing that the wheels were in motion. Once again, hope sprang in his heart that Beth Anne would be back in his arms soon.

*

Early the following morning, Rob pulled up in front of Bill's house. He had no idea what he was going to say to his kids, how to explain where he was going or why. With that on his mind, he walked inside, and saw that everyone was already up, eating breakfast.

Their sad, forlorn faces said everything; the children were missing their mother. Jennifer ate her breakfast in unusual quiet, as she looked up at her father. It hurt Rob to see them unhappy. It was hard to find the right words, because he didn't want to upset them anymore.

"I have to go on a little trip," he said, "but when I get back, Mom will be with me."

Rob, Bill and Susan did their best to calm the kids down. After they had left for school, Rob then spent the rest of the morning packing and making arrangements.

Later in the afternoon, Rob met the kids at the bus stop and walked them home. He tried his best to give them hope, and to speak positively, even though he had no idea what his adventure would entail.

After dinner that evening, Rob read a story to them, before the family watched some T.V. together. After he tucked them in for the night, he sat down in the kitchen, for a cup of coffee with Bill.

"My parents are gonna visit in a few days," Rob said. "It's

fine with me if the kids spend some time with them."

"Whatever they wanna do is fine with us, too," Bill said.

Rob then went on to tell Bill about the $30,000. "I've got to go to the bank in the morning, and withdraw half of it from all of our accounts, including the college fund. I'll either take out a loan for the rest or borrow it from Tex."

"No," Bill said, taking Rob's hand; "let me put the other fifteen up. It's no problem; she's my little girl."

Rob looked at Bill, surprised that they had so much money lying around. "Okay, Bill. But it's only a loan; I will pay you back."

Bill smiled. "Okay, Rob, whatever you wanna call it. But, money means nothing compared to my daughter. I wish I could go with you, but... I know I'd just slow you down. Susan and I will pray for a safe journey, for you and Beth Anne."

Before Rob left for the night, Bill went to his safe and packed the cash in a large envelope, then handed it to Rob.

"Thank you, Bill. Really."

"It's all in there. If you need more, I can wire it to you. Remember, our prayers are with you. And, please be very, very careful."

Rob handed Bill his house keys and a pile of paperwork. "Thanks, again. Can you please hold onto that stuff until we get back? I know you may not want to hear this, Bill, but I've gotta be realistic: if we don't come back, everything goes to our children."

After an uneasy handshake and a goodbye, Rob left in a

hurry.

*

Later that night, Bill was sitting on his front porch, sipping a beer before turning in. It was late, but he couldn't sleep. He had no idea what Rob's plans were, and that was worrying. He knew that whatever it was, it was not going to be easy. But, he had a gut feeling that, somehow, he would see his daughter again.

*

The next morning was cool and clear, without a cloud in the bright, blue sky. Rob had coffee and a quick breakfast, and was at the bank by eight a.m., to withdraw every penny of his savings.

As he left the outskirts of town, he peered in the rearview mirror, wondering if he would ever see his home or his kids again. He was going into the unknown, but he felt better to finally be taking action.

Rob left the interstate, parked his car at the busy terminal center and made his way to the correct terminal for his flight. As far back as he could remember, he had always been fascinated by airports, and after checking his duffel bag, he sat by his gate and watched all the people coming and going. By one p.m., Rob was on his flight to Dallas, with a carry-on full of cash at his side. He took a seat by the window, slipped the bag under the seat in front of him, and tried to relax.

The plane throttled up as it accelerated down the runway, then lifted off. Once they leveled off, Rob grabbed a travel magazine from the seat pocket in front of him, and thumbed through the articles and ads about exotic places. The giant Boeing was loaded with business commuters, most talking about a sales convention in Dallas.

It was a smooth, uneventful flight, and they arrived at the airport right on time. With the bag of cash under his arm, Rob made his way through the crowded terminal, where he was relieved to see the big Texan waiting at the gate.

"Hey, Doc. How was your flight?"

"Okay, Tex," Rob replied, shaking his friend's hand. "I feel a little better now that I'm here and we're actually underway."

They picked up Rob's duffel at baggage claim, and left the terminal for the parking area. It wasn't long before they were headed out of the big city.

"Handles pretty good, huh?" Tex asked of his powerful 4x4. "Rebuilt the motor myself."

Rob smiled and nodded. "I like it, but not as much as my Mustang."

Tex smiled, "I figured you say that, but a real man, he needs a good truck."

They had a good laugh and talked about cars, trucks and motors for a while.

The countryside was wide open and beautiful. There

were miles of white fences along the road, red barns, and herds of horses and cattle grazing in the green, grassy pastures. Here and there, oil-drilling rigs peppered the distant fields of corn and wheat.

After about two hours, they reached Tex's ranch. No one was home when they arrived, except for one of the ranch hands, working out by the barn; Tex had arranged for his wife and two children to stay at her parents' house for a few days.

They walked over to the corral, and Tex called to his horses – some real beauties. He had a close connection with his animals, because they trotted happily over to the fence, one by one, to see him. He petted them and spoke softly to them; it was easy to see how much he loved his pets.

"This here's Missy," Tex said, gesturing toward a small, white horse. "She's a fine girl. Took a while, but I broke her. She's got the touch – yes, sir! This one can turn on a dime." He smiled. "She'd be a good fit for Beth Anne to ride."

Rob managed a smile, as he fed the horses some hay. "You're right, Tex: I'm sure they'd love each other." Overcome by emotion, Rob took a moment to reply, "I pray she gets to ride her."

*

Beth Anne was in her filthy cell, doing her best to rest. As she squirmed to get comfortable on the rickety bunk, there was a bang on the door, and she froze as she looked at the two faces peering through the hatch.

They unlocked the door, and the taller of the two dark-skinned officers stepped inside. He was clearly drunk, and swayed on his feet, with a wild look in his eyes. The other was dressed in a highly-decorated officer's uniform. Both smiled creepily at Beth Anne, as she stood watching them.

The tall man moved closer, then suddenly reached out and grabbed her around the waist with his strong hands. Gripping her, he slid a hand up over her breasts. Beth Anne screamed and tried to pull away. He caught her by the arm. She could smell the alcohol on his breath, as she resisted his efforts. In a flash, he smacked her hard across the face, with the back of his hand, and she found herself on the ground, scurrying to get back onto her feet.

With her face stinging in pain, she bravely stood her ground, and now looked at him with cold defiance in her eyes.

The officer yelled something at her in Spanish, then staggered out and slammed the door behind him. She could hear both men laughing as they left.

Beth Anne tried to calm down. She drank a little water and put a damp cloth on her stinging face, then once again prayed that she would see her family again.

*

Tex led Rob into his large, white-brick house. The rustic

wooden beams and large, red-brick fireplace caught Rob's eye the moment they entered the living room. "Wow, Tex! Your home is beautiful! No wonder you're always talking about your ranch."

Tex walked into the kitchen, then returned to offer Rob a cold beer. "Thanks, Doc. Dad and me put a lot of hard work into this place."

They sat down on the brown leather sofa, to go over every minute detail of their upcoming mission.

"There's been a chance of plans," Tex announced, as he opened a large map: "now we're going to catch a flight to Bogotá, then take a taxi to the train station. From there, we'll hop on a train and head north to the Caribbean coast; we'll end up in the city of Cartagena. My contact will rendezvous with us at the train station and give us a lift to a small harbor town on the coast." Tex stopped to light up a smoke, then continued: "Then, we'll take a boat ride, to an isolated area a little farther north. There, we'll pick up some of our weapons, then wait for the chopper; the heavy gear will already be on board."

"How long will we have to wait?" Rob asked.

"I figure they'll pick us up around sunset, and drop us off at a predetermined point, about three miles southeast of the base."

"Sounds good – even though I hate riding in those damn choppers," Rob replied.

Tex was on the phone for another hour, finishing off all the arrangements, so they could head out early in the morning. Once all was set to go, Tex poured them one of his special drinks. Rob took a sip and shuddered; it was strong, but smooth and warming as it went down.

Tex held his glass up: "Here's to a safe journey for us all. May we find your beautiful lady!"

Rob lifted his drink and clinked the glass against his friend's. "Yes, my friend; I pray that we find Beth Anne alive and break her free from those animals who have her."

The ranch hand came in, with a great-smelling tray full of food. Tex introduced the two men to each other. Will was a small, rugged type, with a handlebar mustache; he was a great cook, and they didn't hesitate to dig into the warm biscuits, barbecue, and homemade pork and beans, as they sat out on the back porch. Tex smiled as he ripped through a rib; "Old Will sure can make some grub, huh?"

"You got that right, Tex; this sauce has just the right bite to it," Rob said, looking up at the stars in the clear, night sky. He'd never seen them so vividly – so big and bright – and that warmed his soul as much as the food warmed his belly. He hoped that, somewhere, Beth Anne was looking up at those stars, too, knowing that he was thinking about her, and was on his way to save her.

Before turning in, they finished their drinks by the fire and talked more about the mission. Rob handed Tex the bag of money. "It's all cash, in small bills," he said.

Tex lit a Marlboro and set the bag down beside him. "This'll take care of it, Doc. If not, I'll cover the rest."

Rob and Tex shook hands. "I could never pull this off

without you, Tex. I don't care about the money; I'd sell my soul for her."

"I know, buddy; that's why we're here. Lucky for us, we've got that intel from Agent Sweet Thing and my contacts from a prior mission, so we've now got a workable plan."

"Yeah, it is a great plan," Rob replied. "By the grace of God, we're going to get her out."

Tex smiled. "That's right, Doc. Now, let's get us some sleep; we're facin' a mighty big day tomorrow."

*

In another corner of the world, Beth Anne huddled in a small, filthy blanket she found in her cell, and finished the last of the stale bread and water they gave her. She did not feel at all well; she was suffering from a terrible headache and cold chills.

After she ate, she leaned back on the hard, wooden bunk and fell asleep, to the sound of noisy guards drinking and playing cards just outside her cell. Throughout her fitful sleep, she dreamt of Rob and her children, and she wondered if she would ever see any of them again.

*

The next morning, Rob and Tex were up early.

They had their coffee on the porch, looking out at the

tall grass, swaying in the breeze. Streams of sunlight from the horizon tickled the countryside with a golden glow, and the air was fresh and clean, with just a hint of the earthy aroma of cut grass in it. In the corral, the horses were at the troughs, and pulling at the hay bins for their morning feeding. Deep in thought, Rob bowed his head and silently prayed for his wife, asking the Lord to help them in their journey into the darkness.

Tex put his hand on Rob's shoulder. "You're so quiet, Doc. You okay?"

"Yeah, I'm alright, Tex; I was just daydreaming. I'm ready to roll whenever you are."

Chapter 5
HARM'S WAY

They arrived at the busy airport terminal around eight in the morning, and checked in at the airline counter. Tex led the way through the crowd then, when they reached their gate, he wandered off to fetch something to eat at the snack bar. Rob sat down in the waiting area to read the newspaper, again caught up in his fascination with airports – so many people coming and going, to and from places all over the world.

After an hour or so, they heard their boarding call and finally settled into their seats. The big jet taxied into position, throttled up and thundered down the runway, and they lifted off into a steep climb. The pilot punched in the coordinates for their southward journey to Bogotá, Colombia.

Much to their surprise, Rob and Tex were almost alone on the jumbo jet, with plenty of room to spare. Tex ordered some drinks and they watched a movie, then the Texan found an empty row of seats and stretched out for a nap.

Rob finished his drink and sat back, listening to the endless humming of the jet engines. He thought about his family, and prayed they would all be together again soon. His mind filled with questions and what-ifs about their mission, and about Beth Anne, until the lullaby of flight coerced him into sleep.

A few hours later, the pilot started the approach for the airport, turned on the seatbelt signs and prepared for landing. The flight attendant stirred Rob and Tex from their snoozing, as the plane began to turn and descend. Still half-asleep, they fastened their seatbelts and looked out of the windows; they could hear the hydraulics of the landing gear, as the wheels locked into their downward position with a clank. Slowly, they continued their descent through the puffy, white clouds.

Rob was overcome by a strange feeling, as he scanned the tropical landscape below; it reminded him of Vietnam. The jet banked into a wide turn over the trees, then floated over the runway and landed.

It took about an hour to taxi to the gate, get through customs and pick up their packs from baggage claim. When they finally walked out of the airport, it felt as if they had stepped into an entirely different world.

It was a tropical destination, with palm trees and brightly-colored flowers all around, but both men knew that it was certainly no paradise. The humid air had a warm, earthy scent to it – one which reminded Rob of when he had first met Beth Anne, while she was serving as a nurse, at a field hospital in Vietnam.

They walked over by the taxis and waited. Downtown Bogotá was a busy place, full of people, with cars and buses moving in every direction; it took a while, but finally a cab pulled up to the curb.

Tex opened the door and handed the driver some cash. "When does the train leave for Cartagena?"

"Cartagena? The train?" The driver looked at his watch. "One hour," he replied, in broken English. They got in and he pulled into traffic.

Rob and Tex sat back and took in the scenery of the all-too-foreign place. Bright, white stucco buildings and tall palms lined the road, as they left the airport area. They passed an open-air market, before the driver made a sharp turn onto a winding, red-brick road. When the train station came into view, a few minutes later, the driver pulled into the taxi-stand and let them off at the gate.

They grabbed their bags and headed up the stairs to the loading platform, where they got in line at the ticket window, sweating as the intensely hot sun beat down on them.

Tex wiped his brow; "It's been a long time since I've felt heat like this."

Rob wrinkled his nose at the sweat beads which formed on his face. "We should get some water before we board that train."

They bought two one-way tickets to Cartagena, then found a seat in the shade. Rob found a refreshments stand next to the ticket booth, where he bought some water, a small bottle of rum and two large, ice-cold Cokes. They took their seats under the overhead palms and talked about the trip.

Out of the corner of his eye, Rob noticed a man smiling at them – a Hispanic stranger, tall with long, black hair and a neatly trimmed beard. Rob gave Tex a nudge with his elbow, as the man slowly walked toward them.

"You are Americans, no?" he asked, with a smile. "May I interest you in something special for your trip?"

They both stared in surprise, as the man opened his briefcase to reveal packets full of white powder and bags of what appeared to be marijuana.

Tex smiled as he lit one of his cigarettes. "Not today, thanks, my friend. We're here on business."

The man's expression and tone changed immediately. "Oh, I am sorry to hear that," he replied, with a frown. "What kind of business are you here to do in my country?"

Tex smiled. "We sell boats and marine equipment."

"Oh, yes, of course; I should have known you are a *business*man!" he remarked, and there was something in the way he said it that caught them by surprise. The man closed his briefcase, put his sunglasses back on and turned to walk back to his seat, just as the train pulled into the station.

Rob turned to Tex: "I don't think I like that guy."

Tex smiled. "Me neither, Doc. Let's hope he's not on our train."

With so many commuters bustling about, it was difficult to catch sight of the drug dealer, but Tex spotted him, as he slipped onto the train at the last minute. As Rob followed him to the seats closest to the front doors, Tex lowered his voice to a whisper and said: "That dude's either a crooked cop or a member of the cartel. Worse, I think he's onto us. We've gotta get rid of him, before our cover's blown."

Rob looked toward the rear of the car. "Yeah, the dude gives me a bad feeling, too."

Tex was silent, as the attendant came around to check their tickets. When he had gone, the Texan whispered: "Listen, Doc, if he comes into this car, we'll get up and head to the car in front. You go through the door first, and I'll wait for him behind it."

"Then what?" Rob asked.

"Then... Well, I think I can handle it from there," Tex said, with a grin.

Rob looked back, at just the right moment to see the man coming through the door. "It's go time, friend."

In a flash, they were out of their seats and at the forward-facing door. Tex glanced back over his shoulder and, sure enough, saw the man quickening his pace to get to them. They made their way through the door and stepped onto the short, narrow walkway, where Rob held onto the railing and ran into the forward car. Tex rolled back behind the door, with just enough room between the railing for him to get into position.

The man caught up to them quickly, then reached into his jacket and began to say something. As he stepped onto the walkway, he pulled out a gun, immediately making a beeline for the door. He was in such a hurry to close the gap between he and Rob, he didn't notice when Tex slipped up behind him, locking him in a chokehold, and breaking his neck in one quick, bone-crunching jerk.

The big, powerful Texan then lifted the limp body and threw it over the railing, watching as the corpse rolled into the dense cover.

"Our friend had to leave in a big hurry," Tex panted, when he saw Rob coming back over to him. "Let's go back and sit down. I could use a little drink or two."

Rob's heart was racing so badly, as they took their seats, that he decided to pop one of his nerve pills. Tex took a long pull from the bottle of rum, then handed it to Rob.

Before long, they had finished the bottle and calmed down a little. After a while, Rob drifted off, to the clanking and rocking of the train, as it moved along the rails.

Sometime later, Rob woke to the loud roar of the train whistle, and the feeling of the train jerking as it slowed. Tex was already wide awake, drinking hot, black coffee, and reading a newspaper written entirely in Spanish. Slowly, the train pulled into the station.

As they were disembarking, Tex told Rob: "Watch for a small, Hispanic fella with a cane; he said he'll be wearin' a white linen suit."

"Will do," Rob said, his eyes darting about.

Like Bogotá, Cartagena was beautiful. The colorful flowers and trees were the perfect accompaniments to the white stucco buildings, accented with pastel colors. The place reminded Rob of a colorful painting he had seen at the airport.

They stopped at a corner café, where Rob ordered

himself a tiny espresso. It wasn't long before a small, blue car pulled up to the curb, and the driver got out and waved at them.

"That's our man, Doc," Tex said. "This way; follow me."

The driver welcomed them, and put their packs into the trunk of his little car – which he then drove like a raving maniac!

Once they were away from the train station, the landscape changed dramatically, opening up to rolling plains of green trees and tall grass. They drove for miles, passing farms and gas stations every now and then. At one point, they traveled through a small town, with narrow, cobblestone streets and more white stucco buildings. Then, they came off of the main road and continued along the coast, on a single-lane gravel and sand trail.

Rob inhaled the fresh, salty air through the window – a sign that the Caribbean was near. "You feel it?" he asked, looking over at his friend. "The air is cooler. The sea is nearby."

Tex lit another Marlboro. "Yep, feels good, Doc. We're almost there."

They enjoyed the cool breeze, as they drove along the sandy road. Finally, they came to the rolling surf, and the clear waters of the aqua-blue sea. As they drew closer, they could see sailboats ahead. The place appeared to be a small fishing village, filled with more stucco structures and wooden buildings with metal roofs. Fishing vessels were docked in the harbor, the anglers cleaning and unloading their fish, packing it on ice, and loading their catch into the back of a small truck. Seagulls swarmed the fishing boats, picking at the scraps the workers left behind.

The driver pulled over and stopped alongside the dock, where he unloaded their bags and wished them a safe journey. After Tex gave him a healthy tip, he took off in his little blue Fiat, in a cloud of dust.

Tex and Rob grabbed their luggage and walked onto the dock, to meet their next contact. Rob noticed a man waving to them, from a large, white sailboat at the end of the dock. Tex smiled and turned toward it; "There's our ride."

The thin, gray-haired man spoke fluent English; "Ah, gentlemen, I welcome you aboard my ship." He offered a smile. "Captain Enrico, at your service."

Tex pointed at the very large, very noticeable silver pistol, holstered at his waist. "What's that for, Captain," he asked, "sharks?"

"Of a sort, you could say," Enrico said, never losing his smile. "That, my friend, is just a little insurance." He pointed out toward the sea: "The open water can be a very dangerous place; more than once I've had to use my insurance. Let us pray we won't need it today."

Tex smiled. "Let's hope not, my friend."

They walked on board and followed Enrico below deck. Rob couldn't help but notice the quality interior, crafted from teak and brass, to create an impressive and obviously expensive boat. It was a huge vessel, nice and roomy inside, and it looked to be fairly new.

Enrico poured white wine for all of them from his mini-bar, then pointed to a platter of fried fish and fresh fruit. "Help yourselves," he said, with a smile. He then raised his glass: "Here's to a safe journey, my friends. I hope you find whatever it is you're looking for."

"Believe me, Captain, so do I," Rob replied.

Enrico smiled, as Tex handed him an envelope full of cash. Rob would later learn that Enrico was their main contact, through whom all the arrangements were made.

As the three of them discussed the details of the boat trip, and ate hungrily, Enrico shared some tales of his adventures at sea. Rob could tell how much he loved his boat, and how proud he was of his life on the open water. The fresh food and cold wine helped revive them after their long journey. After the meal, Enrico handed out cigars.

Tex smiled. "Wow, it's been a while since I had a real Cuban cigar."

Enrico smiled as he lit one up. "Only the best Havanas for my guests."

Tex pulled his finely rolled Corona out of the tube and lit it up, but Rob opted to save his for a special occasion – he did open the tube and take a whiff, though; he was relieved to find that they didn't smell anything like Herman's stinky stogies.

Enrico then prepared to cast off. The plan was to take them along the shore, to the pick-up point on a deserted beach, about five nautical miles north. There, the chopper would pick them up to carry them to the insertion point.

Most of their gear was hidden onshore. Tex had thought of every detail; mistakes were not an option.

Once again, Rob felt lucky to know Tex, a man who had so much experience and so many contacts. He was grateful for his buddy's help, and his friendship.

He was also eager to get going; he couldn't stop thinking about Beth Anne, and the promise he had made to his children.

It took quite some time to cover the miles along the coast. To pass time, Tex and Rob sat out on the deck and ate sweet, delicious mangoes, as they watched a pod of dolphins surface and dive in the distance, their silvery, finned backs glinting in the sun.

Finally, the boat slowed, as it passed an old, red buoy and turned inland. Enrico skilfully navigated the sandbars, into a narrow inlet. As he followed the inlet, and slowly moved the boat closer to shore, the calm, crystal-clear water became filled with small, colorful fish, swimming happily across the white-sand seabed. As they drew closer, they saw an old boat beached onshore.

As Rob and Tex stepped out, into three feet of warm, clear seawater, Enrico gathered up their packs. "Good luck, boys," he said, as he handed their packs to them.

Then, he slowly began to back his boat out of the shallows. Once clear, he hit the throttle and powered into a sharp turn, heading back out into open water. Quickly, Rob and Tex hurried ashore and moved across the open sand, into the cover of the palm trees.

Tex scanned the area with his field glasses. "Looks okay, Doc," he surmised. Then he pointed: "Head to that old wreck; our gear should be stashed inside it."

Sure enough, they found three large, plastic tubs amongst the wreck: one was full of weapons; the other two contained an assortment of supplies. They opened up their packs and changed into their camouflage outfits and jungle boots, then checked and loaded their weapons. Tex grinned, as he admired his new sniper setup and his trusty M-16 from 'Nam – Rob noticed that the sleek-looking sniper rifle was camouflaged, to match his outfit perfectly. Rob felt a little safer with a weapon in hand – his own insurance. He'd always appreciated the smooth, lightweight feel of a Mini-16 – lots of firepower in a small package. Each man also strapped on a special HK handgun, with a custom silencer.

"Lookin' good, Doc," Tex said, after giving Rob a once-over. "You look like you've done this before."

Rob smiled. "Thanks; you're pretty impressive yourself, Tex. You look almost darn handsome in green."

The joking and banter helped to break the tension, as did the natural beauty of the place. The palms on the beach were taller than in any of the cities, and the sand was gleaming white. *I'd love to bring my Beth Anne on a vacation to a place like this someday,* he thought, as he gazed at the blue water, and the exotic fish lazily swimming by.

Tex stood and pointed toward the sea: "Look at that, Doc!

Not a good time to go for a swim."

Rob grabbed the binoculars and aimed them at a pair of shark fins, cutting through the surface of the water, in the outer inlet. "Wow! You got that right, my friend. There are two of them bad boys out there; they must be at least ten feet long. What kind are they?"

"Not sure," Tex replied, "think they might be tiger sharks."

They sat by the sea-worn boat, tidying their things up for their mission, and each of them devoured a few chocolate energy bars. It seemed like forever before dusk came, but eventually the light of day began to fade; the orange-red sun cast a bright, golden glow over the cloudless horizon.

Soon, they heard an unmistakable thumping sound in the distance, and the sky filled with blinking lights, just off the coast, as the chopper came in low from the north. Tex grabbed the field glasses; "That's gotta be our ride, Doc."

The 'copter circled over them, then turned and hovered over the beach, stirring up a cloud of swirling sand. As they grabbed their gear and ran for the chopper, more memories flooded into Rob's head: recollections of the rice fields and jungles of Vietnam. *How many times have I jumped on board a waiting chopper, headed into harm's way?* he thought. *Now, after all these years, I'm doing it again.*

Tex smiled as they ran. "Hey, partner, it's just like old times again."

Rob just shook his head, suddenly remembering how much he hated to fly in the damn things.

As their ride touched down, they scrambled to shove their gear on board, then heaved their heavily-camouflaged bodies inside. Tex closed the bay door and they settled in for the ride.

The chopper lifted off and lunged out over the water, gaining altitude as it went into a gut-wrenching turn. Rob felt his stomach churning, as he was slammed back into his seat.

The pilot, a young, Hispanic man, with tattoos covering his muscular arms, spoke English fairly well. "I'm Alex," he said, as the chopper leveled off at cruising speed. As he peeked back at his passengers, he smiled when he noticed the big blade strapped to Tex's leg. "Ah, I see you are a hunter. This place we go is dangerous for hunters." He lit a cigarette and continued: "Not to worry, though; I know the way."

Tex handed him the coordinates for the drop-off, and the two of them discussed the flight plan. Then, as Alex maneuvered the whirlybird low and fast along the coastline, Tex checked his gear again. Rob's stomach felt a little better, but his hands were trembling again. To take his mind off of it, he decided to double-check his gear, too.

Tex handed Rob a small package. "Put some war paint on, Doc; they'll see your pasty-white, smiling face from miles away." Tex then proceeded to apply camo paint to himself, in thick, black stripes under his eyes and splotches of green and brown on his cheeks.

Rob looked at his intimidating friend, the whites of his

eyes glaring out in contrast to the jungle colors – he had to laugh. "Damn, Tex, you look like a big, bad monster!"

The pilot turned for a quick look and burst out in laughter. It was good to laugh; it helped to ease the tension, as they finished decorating their faces and strapping on their backpacks.

"Hang on, my friends!" Alex yelled, a few minutes later. He banked the chopper into a wide turn, then dropped altitude a little, turning the chopper to head farther inland.

They cut over the treetops, still flying fast, over a green valley which opened up to a winding river. The chopper then banked hard to fly upstream, slamming them back in their seats again.

Rob glanced out of the window and saw boats below – presumably just local fishermen. He touched the cross pendant around his neck and, once again, prayed silently: *Please, Lord, let me find her alive.*

Tex yelled, over the roar of the engine: "Say a prayer for us, Alex – I think we're gonna need it."

He then turned to Rob; "You ready, Doc? We're getting close. Lock and load!"

They stood at the ready, by the bay door, waiting for the pilot to signal their drop, as the chopper banked lower. Alex hovered over a small clearing next to the river, where he descended to about five feet. Then, he turned and waved them off, as pieces of chopped grass and dust filled the air, from the rotor wash. Quickly, they dropped their large packs outside, then jumped off after them.

As soon as their feet hit the ground, they grabbed their gear and moved quickly into the tree line, looking for a place to hide in the heavy cover, away from the river. Rob grabbed his weapon and scanned the area, while Tex checked his map and compass settings, to make sure they started moving in the right direction.

The terrain resembled that of Vietnam: hot and steamy, and loaded with insects. They passed around the bug lotion, then proceeded to hack their way through thick jungle, stopping now and then to look around. After an hour of bushwhacking, they found something of a path, where they took a much-needed break.

Rob wiped the sweat from his eyes and took a long pull from his water canteen. "Well, how we doin', Tex? Are we making good time?"

Tex looked around, as he checked his map and compass headings. "If our information is correct, this little trail will eventually lead us all the way up to the cartel post. There should be a stream up ahead; it should be a good hike to get there."

Rob set up the signal transponder, which he hid underneath some brush, by a large rock beneath a recognizable palm tree; when they returned, they would simply have to turn it on and head to the river, from where the chopper would pick them up within an hour.

They followed the trail, stopping now and then to hack through the heavy cover. The trail finally started to open up a bit, but shortly they heard the rumble of thunder in the distance. The moonless sky drew darker and the wind started to pick up.

"Storm's coming," Rob whispered.

As the two of them wisely donned their ponchos, Tex smiled. "Who'da believed the two of us would be sitting in the bush again, wearing these ugly garbage bags?"

"I know, man – and with war paint on our faces!" Rob replied. "It's a weirdly familiar feeling, my friend."

Soon, a torrential downpour and heavy winds were pummeling them. Streaks of lightning filled the distant skyline, occasionally illuminating their way, as they moved under the cover of large trees, huddling there to wait out the storm. In a few hours, the pitch black of night would help them make their final move toward the target.

Rob tried to catch a little shuteye, but he kept thinking about Beth Anne and those nasty terrorists. Still, he finally managed to succumb to the rest his body demanded.

Rob slept peacefully, until quickly snapping awake at the sound of a loud noise – which sounded like the screech of a monkey – in the distance. Everything was dark, but thankfully the rain and lightning were over.

Now the jungle is soaking wet, Rob thought, *it's going to be tough going.*

Tex stirred, as Rob slathered on a thick coating of insect repellant. The mosquitoes were out in full force, so it didn't take Tex long to fully wake up and do the same. "This oughta keep those malaria-carrying bloodsuckers away for a while," he muttered.

Slowly, their eyes adjusted to the darkness. Tex slipped on his night-vision headset and looked around. They gathered the rest of the gear, checked the map and compass headings, then slipped once again into the unknown. Rob's pack contained a mini-flashlight, med-kit, smoke grenades, extra clips and other assorted necessities; Tex was weighed down a little more, with the sniper setup, a claymore and the satchel charges.

On point, Tex turned on his headset and moved out along the trail, gesturing for Rob to follow him. Rob's senses were on high alert, as he moved into position behind his friend, into the dark, unforgiving jungle.

Their plan was to follow the winding trail, until they came to the stream. From there, they would follow uphill to the north, then push on until they reached what the map showed to be a big lake. They would circle the lake, then find a good hiding spot, close enough to the cartel camp to watch and wait. With a little luck, they should make it to the lookout by daylight.

The rain and clouds departed, and the night sky began to clear; thankfully, too, it was starting to get cooler. After an hour of sloshing through the wet cover of the overgrown trail, Rob could finally see the quarter-moon in the starlit sky above. Tex continued onward, still wearing his night-vision headset.

The trail opened up a little more, and they moved along it at a quicker pace. Unfortunately, they had to stop now and then, to hack through portions of the old trail, but they pushed and climbed onward, making good ground.

Suddenly, Tex stopped, signaled hold and waved Rob over. "There," he pointed. "Can you hear it, Doc?"

Rob listened closely, as he caught his breath. "Sounds like rushing water to me."

They moved in the direction of the noise, then Tex stopped again, checking his map. "Good news, buddy," he whispered: "according to the map, that waterfall we're hearin' is fed from the lake above."

"Good," Rob replied. "We're getting closer – I am sure of it."

Soaking wet and totally exhausted, they finally reached the stream at the base of the waterfall. There, they took a moment to drink from their canteens, then refilled them with the fresh water from the falls. Tex took off his headset and dipped his head in the cool, clear water; Rob was right behind him for a refreshing dip. Tex sat down on a mossy boulder and broke out some rations.

"We made four miles in good time, considering the shape of the trail," he said.

Rob swallowed and looked over at him. "I don't know about you, but my feet are soaking wet and my legs are killing me. We're not as young as we used to be."

"You're tellin' me, partner," Tex said, as he lit up another Marlboro. "Just think, we used to do this stuff every day in 'Nam!"

"That's right," Rob replied, "but that was a long time ago."

They ate and reminisced for a while, looking at the forest

around them.

"Darn pretty, the way that water flows over the side," Tex said.

It took a moment for Rob to reply, as he tried to take it all in: "It sure is."

In spite of the ugliness of the cartel living all over the place, the beauty of nature here was spectacular. It was a dreamy sight, the way the water cascaded down over the rocks above, forming a lagoon which reflected the moonlight. The sound of the water, accompanied by the chorus of the jungle creatures, should have been soothing, but Rob was having trouble appreciating it – or anything else: Beth Anne and her safety were the only thing on his mind. He could picture her now, terrified and helpless, in the hands of those filthy, drug-dealing terrorists. Of all of the hellish things he had gone through in life, this was the worst, and it was tearing him apart.

"You okay, buddy?" Tex asked, trying to snap him out of it.

"Yeah, I'll be okay," Rob said, jolted from his vision. "Truly, though, this whole mess is getting to me, Tex – especially now that we're close. I pray we find her alive. I'm trying not to think of the dark forces holding her in their evil grip. If things go wrong, and our mission turns out... bad..." He paused, unable to say the words. "I know one thing, my friend: if anything happens to her, I will take as many of those animals down with me as I can. You don't have to go in, Tex; just set me up and back me from a distance with your rifle."

Tex took out his knife, its long, razor-sharp, steel blade glistening in the moonlight. "I didn't bring this baby along for nothing. You will have your revenge, and we'll get her out of this place. Just stay positive and focus on the mission."

Rob's little bit of hope was what kept him going; if anyone in the world could help him rescue her, it was Tex. He silently thanked God for his friend – a loyal companion, in some of his most difficult moments. He could still remember his time in action with Tex, one of the most revered snipers in Vietnam. On one occasion, the entire platoon was hit hard, pinned down behind enemy lines, and stuck between the crossfire of two or more V.C. snipers; with legendary skills, Tex silently slipped into the jungle and, within a few hours, the unmistakable sound of his sniper rifle rang out several times. The platoon checked for all-clear, waiting for Tex to come back, but they had no choice but to move out. Then, the next morning, Tex walked back into camp, grinning from ear to ear, with several enemy rifles slung over his shoulders.

It was time to move on, so Rob and Tex began their treacherous climb up the waterfall. The rocky footing was slick with mist, and it was slow going. When they finally reached the top, they came upon another old, overgrown trail. As they pushed ahead, Rob noticed the land was almost flat.

Tex signaled for a hold and peered through the trees

ahead, to the place where the moonlight was glistening on the water. With the lake in sight, they slowly and quietly moved in that direction. Tex slipped his sniper rifle out of its case, scanning the area around the lake with his night-vision scope. "We got nothin', Doc; no lights or movement."

Rob took the rifle and had a look around. "We'd better be careful. We're getting closer, Tex – I can feel it."

They discussed their plan for a moment, deciding it would be best to move east, follow the trail and slowly circle the lake. Their pace was much slower as they moved uphill again, and Tex stopped often to scan the area ahead.

Near the other side of the lake, Tex signaled hold again. He heard a noise in the distance: the sound of moving vehicles. Quickly, they crawled to find better cover. Tex looked around, as the noise grew gradually louder. "Looks like a road up there, Doc."

The sight of headlights bobbing in the distance confirmed his suspicion. They waited in the cover, as a convoy of freight or supply trucks rumbled past them and out of sight.

"Must be a private driveway," Tex said; "I don't see it on the map. Those trucks are probably loaded with drugs or weapons, headed for the cartel base. We'd better get outta here, before someone spots us."

"Roger on that, Tex; it doesn't feel right here," Rob said. He quickly checked the compass and map again. "What do you think? Should we move parallel to the lake, now that we're on the other side?"

Tex smiled. "Roger that; I was just thinking the same thing. We need to stay between the lake and the road."

They moved quickly along the hillside, for what seemed like forever. Rob's legs burned, and sweat poured into his eyes. But, no matter how much his muscles hurt, or how bad the stinging in his eyes, he would never stop following the big Texan leading the way.

Finally, they reached a small clearing, and Tex again signaled hold, as he wiped the sweat from his forehead. "The only good thing about goin' uphill is that we'll be heading downhill all the way back."

"Amen to that," Rob added, as he poured some water over his face.

Slowly, they started across the grassy clearing, keeping the lake to their right and the road to their left.

Their pace gradually slowed, as Tex looked around them, through his headset. After a while, he pointed: "There! See it, Doc? The sky's much lighter to the east. It has to be coming from the base."

Rob's heart jumped. "Damn, Tex, I hope we found it. Finally, this nightmare has an end in sight."

They moved on, keeping low and slow, to get a closer look.

Then, again Tex signaled. "This looks good," he said, pointing to the outline of the base.

They were slightly elevated, in a small cluster of trees which offered heavy cover. From their vantage point, about 150 yards from the base perimeter, they could see everything. Finally, the long, uphill hike was over. They were tired and out of breath, having pushed themselves to the limit. Rob opened his pack and guzzled some water, and Tex handed him another Power Bar.

After a well-deserved break, Tex showed Rob how to cut and use the vegetation as camouflage. By the time he had finished his landscaping exhibition, even though he was standing no more than ten feet from Rob, it was very hard to see him, even in the moonlight.

From their lookout, they saw headlights, as more trucks came and went, exiting and entering through the road at the rear of the base.

Tex stretched out on the ground. "Doc, we may as well try to get a little rest. It will be light in two and a half hours."

"Hey, Tex, you know something? You're the only one who calls me Doc," Rob said.

Tex smiled. "It just fits you. Besides, Doc, I didn't stuff that med-kit in your gear for nothing."

"Well, I still call you Tex; it's a good fit for you, too, my friend."

They settled in, but Rob had trouble sleeping, still plagued by worry about the love of his life. He had started to fear that she might not be alive when they found her, but all he could do was wait, hope and pray. Time seemed to stand still, as anticipation and fear closed in around him. Finally, though, his mind gave in to his body's demands, and sleep took him once again – albeit filled with dreams of the beautiful woman he hoped to save.

Chapter 6
HIT AND RUN

Tex began to stir, as the yellow-orange glow of the sunrise started to extinguish the night. He got up and scanned the base, with the high-powered scope on his sniper rifle: it was quiet, with no movement to speak of. He turned to Rob, who was still out cold, and tapped him on the shoulder; "Get up, partner. It's look-and-learn time."

Rob jerked awake, then blinked in the glare of the rising sun. "Damn, Tex. I can't believe I finally passed out."

"Yeah, well, if anybody needs his beauty sleep, it's you," Tex teased.

They ate some rations, shared some water, then waited for more daylight, while Tex fine-tuned their camouflage a little. The golden sunlight was just filtering through the canopy of tree cover, as they slowly crawled into position, to get a better look with the field glasses.

The first thing they noticed was that the cartel base was not as big as it had appeared in the night. A high chain-link fence topped with barbed wire surrounded the entire perimeter, and in the middle was a large metal building, with a loading bay. The road entered from the front and circled around to the back of the base. By the front entrance was a small gatehouse, occupied by a single guard;

to the west, there stood a watchtower, around thirty feet tall, housing one guard – his weapon was resting against the doorframe. The guard at the gate was sitting in a chair, his attention squarely on whatever it was he was reading.

Just behind the watchtower was a smaller building, made of cinderblock, with a metal roof. They crawled a little closer for a better look, noticing that there was a single metal door on the cinderblock building, along with a few very narrow windows. A separate chain-link fence ringed with barbed wire surrounded it.

Tex smiled. "That's the place, my friend. If they brought your girl here, she's probably in there."

Rob's heart lightened. "She is in there, Tex – I know it; I can feel it in my bones, man."

"We have to find a way to slip inside. I know it looks rough, but we'll get the job done."

They watched for hours, crawling around the base perimeter to recce. By noon, everything was getting hot and steamy. When they spotted a large fuel tank behind the main building, Tex moved in for a closer look.

"They must have over a hundred gallons of diesel in there," Tex said, once he was back in the cover. "I figure—" Suddenly he trailed off, signaled for a hold and slowly drew his blade.

In one quick slash, he reached over Rob's head and brought his blade down, hard.

Rob rolled back in shock, as the enormous black-and-yellow snake did its final dance. "Damn, Tex," he said, as the hairs stood up on the back of his neck, "I didn't even see that thing."

Tex grinned, holding up his blade, with the snake's bloody head stuck to the tip of it. "I musta passed by it myself; lucky for us, I just happened to look back at the right time. This nasty bugger is poisonous."

"It's good to have a little luck on our side, today of all days," Rob replied, with a smile. "Thank God for Texans with big knives!"

Tex wanted to laugh, but he held it in, knowing that they had to be as quiet as possible. They looked around for a while longer, then crawled back to the lookout, once they were confident they'd seen enough.

Tex pulled his knife out again and used it to scratch a makeshift map into the dirt, doing his best to mark the layout of the base. "This is how it'll go down, Doc. As I'm sure you noticed, these dudes aren't military; none of them are in uniform. Also, lucky for us, I didn't see any F.A.R.C. rebels. The cartel guards are a little laid back, and that guy in the tower was napping half the time; that'll work to our advantage. They work on a two-hour rotation, from the gate to the lockup, then to the tower," he said, pointing at the base.

Rob was impressed. "Wow, you really know what to watch for, Tex,"

"Before you go into a snake pit, Rob, you gotta know what kind of vipers you're dealing with!" Tex said. "We'll leave most of the heavy weapons behind and go in light, with just our handguns and the bare essentials. We'll make our move straight to the wire, then slip in at the base of the tower, right after they rotate. Since it all starts with the dude in the tower, we'll take him out first, as soon as he comes down. Then we hide, so we can give his relief a little surprise party when he shows up; you'll do a wardrobe change then go to relieve the guard at the lockup gate. In the meantime..." he paused, to point at his pack of satchel charges and claymores, "...I'll be busy doing a little home wiring. The big one goes under that diesel tank; it'll be quite the fireworks display!"

Rob smirked, doing his best not to reveal the fear he felt. "Sounds good to me, buddy. The fireworks will create the diversion we need to get a good head start, on the way out. I'm just not too sure about me, Tex."

"What do ya mean, partner?"

"Well, for starters, how in the hell am I going to just walk up to that guard in disguise? What if he rumbles me straight away? I sure hope I don't blow it." Rob was increasingly unable to hide the trembling of his hands.

Tex handed the water canteen to him. "Let's think about this for a minute," he said: "I'd pop the guard at the lockup myself, but I'm way too tall; you, on the other hand, are just about the right size and build."

"I guess so," Rob said.

"Hey, let's take a little break," Tex said, handing Rob a couple of Power Bars. "We'll lose it out here in this heat, if we don't take time to eat and drink."

Rob realized that Tex was right. As soon as he had something in his stomach, he felt a whole lot better – even braver, too, somehow.

Tex continued: "Just act like they do; watch 'em and learn. Walk up calmly, laid back like they do, then put one in his head with your sidearm. Then, open the gate and get outta sight. From there, it's your call. Whatever happens, though, wait for me; I will come to you, and we'll head into the lockup together. Try to stay calm, 'cos I'm gonna need you to back me up. The whole deal has to go down quick; stealth, confidence and surprise are the keys, just like in 'Nam. Once we make our move, it won't be long before the jig's up and the bad guys come after us."

"Yeah, fast and quiet – I know," Rob said, gulping audibly.

"Look, Rob, it probably sounds scarier than it will actually be. We'll find your lady, then get the hell outta Dodge, as fast as our legs will carry us; we'll hustle to that tower, then slip back under the fence. If we get separated, we'll meet back at the falls – from there, it's just a downhill hike back to the pick-up point."

They went through the plan, several times over, until they were sure it was the best possible one they could come up with. Finally, Rob smiled, his confidence restored. "It all sounds good, Tex. Lord willing, it should work. There's no turning back now."

"Right," Tex said, grinning.

Rob looked at the lockup; "I just hope she's on the other

side of that door. I'm going to get her out of here or die trying."

As they waited and watched for the cover of darkness, Rob could only cling to hope, and to the plan they'd come up with. He dozed on and off, with thoughts of Beth Anne and his children constantly drifting through his mind. Once again, it seemed as if time stood still.

*

In her cold, lonely cell, Beth Anne finally gave in to her hunger, nibbling on the stale, moldy bread and sipping the rancid water the guards had given her. She was shivering from fever and the chills. She prayed the bad men would not come for her again. She felt alone and afraid, and was terrified that she would never see Rob, her parents or her children again.

*

Not too far away, Tex heard something and reached for his rifle. "We're about to have company, Doc," he said, as he reached for the field glasses.

Rob jerked awake and listened to the sound in the distance: engine noise, growing louder, as a vehicle rushed down the private road. Before long, a truck passed through the gate and pulled up to the main building, where the back opened and two uniformed men hopped out, along with a woman, who was handcuffed and blindfolded. The men shoved their prisoner, tearing at her blouse as they led her to the lockup.

At the same time, two neatly uniformed men exited the large, metal building. One looked like an officer in his long, black boots and white, wide-brimmed hat. They were laughing about something, as they walked over to the lockup.

Tex smiled, then pulled out his camera and began to click away. "Yes! My man is here!" he said.

"Who?" Rob whispered.

"It seems that there are a few F.A.R.C. rebels to deal with, after all. See that man in the white hat and boots? He calls himself a 'general', but he's really nothing more than a ruthless, murdering, drug-smuggling rebel terrorist – the Colombian government wants to put an end to him and his kind. He'll be my target tonight, and I'm going to take him out, the first chance I get. That'll be big money for us; your thirty grand will be covered, and I'll rake in at least that much, too."

"Why didn't you mention this before?" Rob asked.

"Because I wasn't sure he was here," Tex answered.

Rob put down the field glasses. "I don't care who you take out, Tex, just as long as we find Beth Anne first and we all get the hell out of here!"

Tex continued: "Of course, Doc; she is our first priority. Back home, I asked my sources to dig up some dirt on this cartel, and when his name came up in conversation, they told me he is a big target. These people are ruthless killers, Doc. That self-proclaimed 'general' and his troops are a key part of the well-armed muscle behind the cartel, and they'll sell drugs and weapons to anyone – including other terrorists. They rape and steal from their own people. Lord knows how many lives have been lost in this place – I wanna put a stop to it! I counted five, including him; if we keep things quiet, they shouldn't be a problem. But we've gotta move quick; get in and out before they call for reinforcements."

"You're right, Tex: this is a bad place, full of bad people. The cartel and those rebels are plain evil, spreading their drugs and terror around the world. Tonight, Lord willing, we'll show them the light – and pull Beth Anne out of the darkness. This whole thing reminds me of our time in 'Nam, when we had to fight for our lives."

Tex smiled. "True, my friend. I don't think either of us will ever forget that dark journey."

"Yeah," Rob muttered, his mind once again flashing back to those horrific jungles.

*

Beth Anne huddled in the corner of the cell, unnerved and terrified by the screaming and yelling which came from the next room. She shivered, as she believed that a woman was being beaten and raped on the other side of that wall. She clamped her hands down over her ears, wishing the horrible noise would stop, but it seemed to go on forever.

Thankfully, after a long while she heard a door slam, and the lights went out. Beth Anne rushed to put her ear to the wall; she heard soft crying and whimpering. She wanted to speak to the woman – to try to offer her some comfort – but she was terrified that the guards would hear, and they would come in and torture her. So, instead, she huddled in her shabby blanket and prayed that help would come.

*

Rob and Tex watched the general marching about, barking his orders at the guards. He didn't go back inside the main building, until the last rays of sunlight began to slip over the horizon.

"Almost go time," Tex said.

They concealed their gear, and Tex redecorated his face. He looked like a six-and-a-half-foot alien, as he stood there in his camouflage suit, sharpening his blade. Rob laughed and shook his head. "You know, Tex, you might not need to fire a shot; one look at you might just scare them all to death."

Tex managed to hold back his laughter. "That's the idea, Doc: I *wanna* scare the hell out of them."

An hour after the last rotation, there were no trucks moving in or out, and the loading dock was dark and quiet. When the base's lights came on – just a few lamps, scattered around the dimly-lit buildings – Rob and Tex started their slow crawl, toward the tower. There was just enough light, coming from the buildings, to allow them to find their way around.

When they reached the fence, they used their knives to hollow out a space beneath the wire – it was easy going, in the soft, damp soil. Inside the camp, they crawled to the tower base and set up at the bottom of the ladder. Tex quietly took a charge out of his pack and set it in the tower's frame. Then, they waited.

Before long, they heard their man descending the rungs.

As soon as he set foot on the walkway, Tex silently slipped behind him and, in one quick movement, wrapped his muscular arms around the guard's throat and snapped his neck, with a single, bone-crunching jerk to the left. He eased the dead man to the ground and dragged him out of view.

Rob moved quickly, stripping the corpse of his clothes, then climbed into them. After Tex handed him his sidearm, he chambered a round and clicked on the silencer. *Calm, Rob,* he told himself; *stay calm and think positive.*

A few minutes later, the guard from the front gate showed up, shouldering his weapon as he drew closer. Then, for some reason, the guard changed course at the last minute, and headed right past the area where Tex was waiting for him, walking instead around the tower, in Rob's direction. Rob stayed low, in the shadows of the night, and watched the guard approach; slowly, with his weapon drawn, Rob moved toward him. Before the guard even knew it, Rob shot him in the middle of his forehead – thanks to the silencer, there was little more noise than a soft "pop".

Tex dragged the dead guard under the tower and grabbed his pack. "Just stay cool, Doc. You can do this! I'll be right behind you, after I place the other charge underneath the fuel tank and set up the claymores, to cover our retreat."

Before Rob could reply, Tex had already slipped around the tower and disappeared into the night.

Rob placed his pistol in his waistband behind his back, grabbed the guard's weapon and walked confidently toward the lockup. He shouldered the rifle and tried to imagine himself as the terrorist, forcing himself into a slow, easy, laid-back gait. He tilted his hat at just the right angle to hide his face; luckily, the guard's clothes fit him fairly well. The man sitting outside the lockup didn't even notice what was coming his way. Rob's heart thundered in his chest, in anxiety and anticipation, as he drew closer.

By the time the guard suddenly did look at him, registering surprise, it was too late for him: Rob's pistol was out and pointing at him; the guard's face twisted with momentary fear, an instant before the bullet tore into his forehead. The force of the impact knocked him backward, right off his chair, and Rob made quick work of dragging him through the gate, out of sight.

He walked over to the building and sat down in the corner, by the door. His adrenalin rippled through him, when he suddenly realized that he was finally in the very building where Beth Anne was being held. He had to forcefully will himself to stay calm, and to wait for Tex.

After a while, Rob's impatience and excitement got the better of him. He scanned the base, looking for some shadow or silhouette to indicate that his friend was coming, but he saw no movement. He trusted Tex, and knew that his friend was busy setting the place up to blow, but still he couldn't stop his hands from shaking.

Stay sharp, even though she's in there I need to wait, he told himself, knowing that he couldn't take a nerve pill at the moment.

Finally, Tex emerged from the darkness. "Okay, buddy, let's get rolling!" he whispered. "Just remember to check your fire."

The next few minutes seemed to pass in slow motion...

Tex grabbed the door handle and swung into the room, with Rob right behind him, his sidearm drawn and at the ready. The guard, surprised by the sudden invasion, jumped from his desk chair and reached immediately for the phone, but Tex was on him in an instant; he made quick work of slashing the man's throat with his big, steel blade; blood splattered against the wall, as Tex held his hand over the guard's mouth, to keep him from trying to scream. Within seconds, Tex eased the guard to the floor, and the life drained out of his victim. Tex drew his own sidearm.

Meanwhile, Rob sensed movement to his right: another guard, bursting through the doorway. Before Rob could turn and fire his weapon, the guard had grabbed his hand, and was trying to gain control of the pistol. Tex watched them fight for the gun, trying to get his own clean shot at the guard, but to no avail. Locked in a life-or-death struggle, the two men went crashing over the desk. Then, as they fought for the gun, a shot rang out.

Tex winced in pain, as the bullet snagged his upper arm, but still he moved in to help his friend. Rob lifted his knee, driving it hard into the guard's groin, then lunged for his gun, as it fell out of his hand and hit the floor.

*

Beth Anne heard the commotion and the gunshot. Not knowing what was happening, she could only stand there in terror.

Maybe they're coming to shoot me now!

*

The guard was still keeling over, crying out from the blow to his crotch, when Tex knocked him back against the wall, with a stiff kick. With that, Rob moved in, leveled his gun and fired twice: *pop-pop!* The impact sent the guard hurtling against the wall and, just like that, his fighting days were over.

"Is that bad?" Rob asked, gesturing toward Tex's arm.

"Nah, just a flesh wound, partner," Tex said with a grin;

"I'll be okay."

"Good." Rob popped a fresh clip into his sidearm.

They heard noise behind them, as they approached the black steel door.

"Damn," Rob muttered, as he tried the door and realized it was locked.

Quickly, they checked the guards for keys, and Tex smiled when he found them in the bloody pocket of one. "Here!" he said, tossing the bunch to Rob with his good arm.

Rob moved toward the door, then paused for a moment, as he heard a noise behind it: that of a woman's sobbing. He prayed it was his Beth Anne, and the idea excited him so much that he could barely manage handling the keys. Finally, the door opened and his heart leapt.

There, sitting in the corner, with a terrified look on her face, was the woman he had come to find.

"Rob?" she gasped. A smile began to curl her lips, when she saw him standing in the doorway. "Is it really you? Oh, my god!"

They embraced, in a flood of emotion.

"Thank God! Beth Anne, I thought I'd lost you! I just—"

"Y'all are gonna have to save your hanky-panky for later," Tex interrupted; "right now, we gotta move out."

Rob was so caught up in the moment, he hadn't even thought about the other woman, but her screams from the next room suddenly caught his attention. Quickly, they opened the door to her cell. She was standing in the center of the room, crying and mumbling in Spanish as they neared her. Rob immediately recognized her as the woman they had seen being pulled out of the truck.

"I was sure they were going to kill us both," Beth Anne said, trembling. "Thank God you came for me!"

Rob examined Beth Anne and the other woman. Both had blood on their clothes and bruising on their faces and arms; they were both pale and shaken. He smiled as he gently took his wife's hand. "Well, it's going to be okay now, Beth Anne; we're here to take you out of this evil place."

Tex heard a lot of noise coming their way, and started pacing around the doorway, like he always did in 'Nam when he was anxious. "Let's go, people; we gotta move! I'm sure they're sending the welcome wagon."

Both women walked over to embrace Tex.

Tex smiled. "Ladies, we can talk later. Right now, we have to get the hell outta here, while it's still clear. Stay in line and keep low. We'll move straight to the tower and out through the wire."

As Rob glanced down at Tex's hand, he saw a river of red running down it, dripping onto the cement. For a few seconds, an image from long ago flashed through his mind: that of wounded men in need of bandages. He knew his friend needed patching up, but his medical kit was still in his pack, back at the lookout.

Tex and Rob hurried the women into the camouflage ponchos from their packs, then guided them out, coaching them quickly toward the tower. They followed the shadows along the walkway, reaching the wire in no time. Tex turned to look at the base once more, and saw flashlights moving around in the darkness. Quickly, they ran into the bush, heading back the way they had come.

They briefly stopped at the lookout, where Tex hurried to set up the sniper rifle, while Rob changed out of the guard uniform and grabbed his med-kit.

"They're havin' a good look around," Tex said, examining the camp through his night-vision scope. "Won't be long before the jig is up. We gotta go – now!"

Rob grabbed the Texan's big, rough hand. "You're not going anywhere, my friend, 'til I check out that arm."

Tex sighed. "Okay, Doc, but make it quick." Tex winced in pain, as Rob ripped his shirtsleeve open, before continuing: "I need to create a diversion, before they pick up our trail."

Rob cut away part of the sleeve, then carefully checked the wound: a deep, gaping hole in Tex's bicep.

"You're lucky it missed the bone," he said, motioning for Beth Anne to keep pressure on it. "This might sting a little," he added, as he applied some disinfectant and bandaged it tight. He then handed Tex a water bottle and some meds, advising: "Take these to prevent infection."

Tex smiled. "Hey, Doc, it's like old times again, ain't it?"

Rob smiled back, as he packed up his med-kit. "Well, I hope this is the last time we gotta deal with bullets and bandages, my friend."

"Thanks, Doc. It feels better already," Tex said. "Look, you know the way back; y'all go on ahead, at the double, 'fore things get busy around here." He pointed down the trail: "Make your way back down there, all the way to the falls. I'll meet you there, after I take care of the 'general' and his pack of rats."

Rob wanted to argue, but he knew it was no use: Tex was serious, and he was not a man to be bargained with. So, he grabbed his pack, secured his sidearm and picked up the Mini-16. "Okay Tex, but don't be long."

"I won't, Doc. But, if I'm not there by dawn, don't wait on me; just get yourselves to that pick-up site and turn on the transponder."

Rob nodded, instructing the ladies what to do.

But, before they could leave, bright lights illuminated the whole base area.

"Get out of here now!" Tex yelled. Then, he moved into position, shouldered his sniper rifle and started firing at the base. The booming blasts of the big rifle echoed all around the hillside.

Rob, on point, led the women back through the bush, keeping the beam of his small flashlight low. After some searching, he found the trail, and they headed downhill at a brisk pace.

After they had moved a good distance away, Rob stopped to look behind them, to see if they were being followed. There was suddenly a bright, white flash of light, as a huge explosion engulfed the tower. "Everyone down! Hit the dirt!" he yelled, grabbing Beth Anne to shelter her.

The ground shook, as the shockwave blew over them.

Then, they heard Tex's gunfire, followed by one explosion after another. Rob was relieved that Tex had got the opportunity to set off the charges which would send the cartel base into total chaos.

"My god, Rob; I hope Tex is okay," Beth Anne said, as they stopped for a moment.

"He's good. I just hope he gets on his way soon. Let's keep movin," Rob said, determined to get to the falls.

Beth Anne and the Colombian woman kept pace, running for their lives, with the moonlight revealing the way. Rob had to focus hard to find the proper route, and he stopped occasionally to check his map and compass headings, fully aware that they couldn't afford to get lost. Once he was confident they were heading in the right direction, they all took off again. Soon, they were far enough away from the base that they could make better use of the flashlight.

Suddenly, a huge, ground-shaking explosion erupted from the base, and the trio instinctively got down and looked back, to see a huge, yellow-orange fireball rising into the air. A hot draught rushed past them, from the powerful force of the blast as the fuel tank went up.

"C'mon," Rob said. They took off toward the falls again.

Finally, Rob found signs of the tracks they had made on the way in, and it was a relief to have visible confirmation of their location. Once they reached the trail to the falls, they started to make good time, moving along and descending the hillside.

Now a good distance from the cartel base, they shared some water. Then, Rob opened his pack and gave the ladies some blankets and Power Bars. Starving, they gobbled up the bars, one after another.

Beth Anne noticed Rob's hand shaking, as he took in a long gulp of water from the canteen. "I'm so proud of you, Rob," she told him. Then, she asked: "How are the kids?"

Rob pulled her close and kissed her. "They're fine; they're just worried about you. The whole town is, in fact; everyone's been looking for you. They'll all be relieved to see you again – me most of all," Rob said, with a tear forming in his eye.

"Not half as relieved as I am to see you," she said, wearing a gorgeous smile which he would never forget.

With a sheepish smile of his own, Rob again picked up his pack and rifle. "Sorry to cut our little picnic short, ladies, but we'd better get moving," he said.

Once again, the trio moved on.

Before long, they were starting to make their way around the lake. Rob stopped now and then for the women to rest, while he looked anxiously back up the trail for Tex.

Chapter 7
SILENT STALKER

Back at the camp perimeter, Tex left the lookout and crawled back into the heavy cover. With his night-vision headset on, he crept silently, expertly becoming one again with his surroundings.

He found the charge placed at the tower, in the crosshairs of his night-vision scope, and squeezed off a shot; then, he ducked behind a downed tree, as the explosion ripped over him.

Tex moved quickly around the blast area, his senses on edge as he searched for his target. He saw movement toward the rear of the base, but it was difficult to get a clear view, through all the smoke billowing from the fires. The watchtower and main building were in ruins, and men were running about everywhere, trying to put the fires out.

As the reverberation of the blasts rocked the whole area, a few miles north of the base, the rebel garrison came to life.

*

The garrison leader – the general's younger brother, Armand – looked out toward his cartel camp in dismay and disbelief, shaking his head at the eerie, orange-yellow glow in the sky. "The base is on fire! We are under attack!" he shouted, before starting to run around frantically, barking orders at his men.

The rebels, shocked and fearful, ran for their weapons and ammo, as another blast rocked the area.

After Armand gathered his own gear, he managed to get all of his men in line, running to board their trucks to head for the base.

*

Tex made his way around to the rear of the camp and scanned the area. Men were scurrying all over, trying to put out fires, but he saw no sign of the general. At first, he thought the man might already be dead.

But, then another look through his night-vision scope told him otherwise; there, in amongst a group of guards, the general was darting about, pointing and yelling orders. Tex dialed in the scope settings for a 200-yard shot, then waited for the right moment.

Finally, the general held for a second, to order his troops into a large truck. *Now or never,* Tex thought, as he steadied the big rifle and braced himself for the shot. Moving the crosshairs over his unsuspecting target, he took a deep breath and exhaled, as he waited for just the right feel of the trigger.

Boom!

The blast jammed the rifle into his shoulder, as the bullet

reached maximum velocity. The general was still shouting when the bullet ripped into his head. A perfect shot, from 200 yards away.

Tex fired a few more times with the rifle, picking off troops as they scrambled out of the truck. Then, he stopped firing and quickly moved, before anyone could get a clear bearing on his location.

He found a good vantage point, at the base of a tree, from where he zoomed in on the last of the satchel charges he had set in place. As men scrambled in his direction, firing wildly, Tex fired at the charge, then quickly dropped to the ground. He smiled from ear to ear, as the shockwaves from the blast ripped over and around him.

One by one, he took down the confused, bumbling troops. Then, when it was safe, he moved back to the lookout, to scan the base once more. The camp was now in total ruins, and the few survivors were tripping over their dead comrades, as they were busily trying to put out the flames.

*

Armand looked out from the open bed of the truck, as it barreled down the road, en route to the base. He had heard the unmistakable boom of a fifty-caliber rifle in the distance.

Suddenly, the lead truck came to a screeching halt, blocked by an enormous, downed tree.

Furious, Armand jumped out of the truck bed. "The enemy is upon us! We must not fail!" he cried, then instantly began yelling for his men to clear the road.

The rebels went to work, frantically hacking and blasting to clear the way. The delay was just long enough for Tex to get back to the lookout, and start preparing for his run to the falls.

Armand and his men jumped off of the truck and looked around at the base, in disbelief. Survivors staggered among the burning buildings, stepping over bodies, embers and debris. "The general is dead," one was saying.

"What?! Come with me – now!" Armand ordered.

With that, his men wandered into the thick smoke, to find whatever was left of the general's body.

Armand jumped back in recoil, when he saw the crude remains of the general; there, in a pool of blood, covered by ashes and dirt, was his brother, all but decapitated by Tex's rifle-shot.

"Who did this?" he demanded, his stomach churning, as the shock and anger erupted inside him. Then, he stepped aside and threw up.

After taking a moment to gather his composure, he turned and yelled to his rebels: "Split up into two groups. Move fast and circle toward the river. Kill them! Kill them all!"

Quickly, the rebels moved out of the ruins and into the bush, with nothing but bloody revenge on their minds.

*

Back at the lookout, Tex gathered his gear and moved out, toward the trail heading to the falls.

He was making good time, when he saw a flicker of light moving in the cover ahead. He kept still and waited, only to then see it again. The third time, the white light was getting closer. Through his night-vision scope he saw flashlight beams and silhouettes moving about the trail, as the rebels searched for them.

Quickly, he slipped into the brush and crawled into the heavy cover, once again becoming one with his surroundings.

Chapter 8
ESCAPE

In her office, Agent Sanders was thrilled when she finally received the call she had been hoping for.

"Gunfire and explosions have been reported at the cartel base," her Colombian contact told her. "I have no further details, but I will update you when more become available."

Though exhilarated, Agent Sanders hung up with a worried frown on her face. The deadline to release the prisoner was less than twenty-four hours away, and she had no idea of Rob and Tex's actual whereabouts. But, at least she now knew they had made it to the base.

*

Back on the trail, Rob and the ladies took another break. Everything had quieted down, and there were no gunfire or muffled explosions heard in the distance. The sky was a strange color: a mix of orange and yellow, tinting the black canopy of night.

God, where are you, Tex? Rob wondered, praying his friend was okay. He tried to convince himself that Tex was on his way, but couldn't help thinking that he should have been here by now. He regretted leaving without him, especially since Tex was wounded. Now, he desperately wanted to go search for him, but he couldn't leave the women behind.

Beth Anne stirred. "Rob, I feel so sick; I've got chills and... Please, please take us away from this place."

Rob immediately noticed how pale and tired she looked; she was covered with cuts and bruises. He placed a hand on her forehead, and was certain that a fever was setting in. "Here, take a couple of these and drink some more water," he said, handing her two more aspirins from his pack and wrapping his blanket over her shoulders.

The Colombian woman didn't look good, either, and Rob gave her some aspirin and water, too. He treated both women's cuts with antiseptic wipes and bandages.

"Do you think they're all dead, Rob?" Beth Anne asked, softly.

Rob checked his compass, as he answered: "I doubt it. But, if they are, they got what they deserved. I don't understand why these people are so nasty. They obviously took you two for a reason, and I'm sure they'll try like hell to get you back. We won't let them, though. I'm gonna get you home."

Beth Anne shivered. "Rob, can't we rest just a little longer? My legs feel so weak."

Rob grabbed his gear. "We don't have much farther to go. I'll help you," he said, wrapping her arm around his waist. "Like I said, they'll come for us, and this time they'll kill us all. Please, we have to keep moving."

Beth Anne nodded. "Alright. I'll be okay, as long as I have you."

Rob checked his watch, as they started toward the falls. "It'll be light in a few hours – that'll make it easier," he said.

It was slow going at times, especially when they had to traverse steep, rocky and overgrown portions of the trail. After the long downhill stretch, they stopped again to rest.

To Rob's surprise, the Colombian woman knew a little English, and managed to introduce herself as Myia. "I am schoolteacher," she said. "Thank you for saving me from cartel animals. They took me; my father very rich, important man in Colombia politics."

While the women rested and recuperated, Rob left them talking for a little while, to scout out the trail ahead.

*

Back up the hill, Tex slipped the silencer onto his sidearm and waited for the flashlights to move closer. There were at least three armed men slowly moving his way, and it did not take them long to close the gap. He allowed them to pass.

As soon as they had, Tex jumped out of the cover like a jack-in-the-box; he shot the first man before the guy even knew what was happening. Then, Tex turned and shot the second, just as he was raising his weapon. He was knocked off of his feet by the third, who pounced on him; his sidearm fell, as they hit the ground hard.

Just in the nick of time, before the man had a chance to

plunge his blade into Tex's chest, Tex managed to grab a grip on his hand. Intense pain shot through his wounded arm, but he held on as, locked in a death struggle, the men fought for control of the blade.

Tex knocked the knife free, by slamming the man's hand against the ground with his good arm. Injured and in pain, the man let go of Tex, and desperately searched for his knife; in one quick motion, Tex jumped on him, drew his own blade, and drove it deep into the man's back. The man let out a horrifying scream; a death cry which echoed through the jungle.

Ignoring the dying man, Tex checked his throbbing arm, which was now once again bleeding profusely. Then, bruised and exhausted, but with a victorious feeling, he gathered his gear. He took a long pull of water from his canteen and hit the trail.

*

Armand's eyes widened, when he and his rebels heard the man's scream in the distance. He pointed in the direction of the sound, as he ordered: "Attack! Kill them all!"

Like a pack of wolves on the hunt, the rebels regrouped and headed downhill.

*

At the bottom of the foothills, Rob and the ladies finally

reached the falls. It was approaching dawn, and the sun was beginning to brighten the eastern horizon, as their ears caught the sound of the rushing water. They moved into the clearing and saw where the river formed into a large pond, before cascading down over the rocky hillside, into the valley below. The sweet, fresh air smelled of water and earth, as the first golden rays of sunlight washed through the mist spraying off of the falls. For a moment, they just sat there, taking in the majestic view.

Rob started to look around, trying to decide on the best way down the slippery, rocky terrain. There was no time to rest and enjoy the scenery.

"Careful, ladies; follow me," Rob warned.

About halfway down, he noticed something moving on Beth Anne's shoulder: a closer look revealed it to be a large, brown, extremely poisonous spider.

"Honey, don't move," he cautioned.

She froze, as he lifted his knife toward her, and flicked the deadly arachnid away. Both women squealed in fear, as they watched the spider scurry under a nearby rock. From that point onward, they both stayed extra close to Rob, as they continued slowly down the falls.

By the time they finally reached the bottom, Rob's mind was racing in different directions. Should he go help Tex or stay with the women? He couldn't think clearly, but this was no time for mistakes. He looked over at Beth Anne and reasoned: *She's still weak, with a slight fever; maybe it would do her good to rest here for a while.*

As Rob looked at Beth Anne, she sat on a nearby rock, sipping water and looking right back at him. Her husband was filthy and sweat-covered, his dirty, brown hair in tangles and his face unshaven. Nevertheless, he was the most handsome man she had ever seen; her hero, the man who had risked his life for her.

Rob shared some more rations with the ladies, then sat down next to his wife and pulled her close, once again. He wasn't sure if she was shivering from fear, fever, or maybe a little of both; he gave her another dose of aspirin, just in case.

Myia walked over and sat down next to them. "She be okay. You go, look for friend. We stay here."

"Thanks. It shouldn't take me long," Rob replied. "Do you know how to use this?" he asked, showing Myia his sidearm.

She smiled. "Yes. Father let me shoot guns."

Rob quickly instructed how to work the safety, then handed the loaded gun over to her. He grabbed his rifle and, without another word, took off to run back up the hillside.

In a small clearing, along the trail, he sought cover and waited, scanning the area with his field glasses. *Please, let me see my buddy soon,* he silently prayed, his hands trembling once again. He did his best to calm down and think positively, as Tex always told him to do. *No pills for me this time; I gotta stay sharp out here.*

Soon, the hillside was basking in full daylight, beneath

the huge, red-orange fireball on the horizon. Still, there was no sign of Tex.

Feeling defeated, Rob walked back up the trail, as far as he dared to go. He remembered his promise to Tex – that if dawn arrived before he was back, Rob would go without him – but in reality that seemed impossible. In the war, when Rob had only himself to worry about, he would have instinctively kept searching for his comrade. But now, his decision was complicated by the two women he had to save.

It's time, he eventually conceded, with a heavy heart; he knew he had to stick to the plan, and go back to activate the transponder, as agreed. So, with burning regret, Rob made his way down to where the two women were.

Beth Anne could see the strain in his eyes, as he answered their questions about Tex. "I... I don't know what happened to him, but I do know it's time for us to leave," he said.

They left the clearing and made their way down toward the river, and it wasn't long before Rob spotted the trail they had used to climb up. Not long after that, they reached the familiar clearing.

Rob searched underneath the palms beside the big rock, and quickly found the transponder. He lifted it out of its container and turned the key switch. The small, green light on the unit began to blink.

Time was running out for Tex now, so Rob ran back toward the falls for one last look, just in case. From the top, his eyes darted left, then right, then left again.

Suddenly, out of nowhere, Tex erupted from the cover, onto the trail right in front of Rob. Nearly startled off of his feet, Rob jumped, his heart pounding.

"Damn, Tex! I didn't think you'd ever come back." Rob grabbed his friend's calloused hand and shook it.

Tex smiled. "Sorry 'bout that. We did good, Doc: the whole cartel base is in shambles; my target, the general, is history; and, you got your lady. Thanks for waiting – even though you disobeyed my instructions," he said, adding: "a few of those F.A.R.C. rebel dudes got in my way."

"Let's get the hell out of this place. I turned on the transponder a short while ago; it won't be long now."

They ran back down the trail and found the ladies, who were both glad to see that Tex had made it out alright. Then, they all worked at a quick pace to gather up their gear, moving closer to the river.

It was a relief to Rob that Beth Anne looked a little better, as she beamed a smile at Tex; her fever had broken. Myia was also doing much better, and she was a big help when it came to hauling all their gear. Everyone quickly got used to her broken English, and she again offered them gratitude for freeing her and bringing her along with them.

"God bless my friends!" she said, as they waited in another clearing, by the river. "My father... he is looking for me. My friends, I pray, and God... He brings you to this bad place to help me."

"We'll get you back to your father," Rob assured her, with a smile.

His smile quickly faded when he noticed blood seeping through Tex's bandages. Once again, he was reminded of 'Nam – a memory that didn't go away – as he grabbed his med-kit, cut off the bloody bandages and applied pressure to the wound. Rob handed Tex his water bottle, as he cleaned and redressed the wound, which appeared to be swollen and infected. "You'll need surgery to clean that mess out and stitch you up properly," he told Tex.

"Aw, Doc, can't I just take two aspirin and call you in the morning?" Tex teased.

Rob laughed, then gave Tex a serious look; "'Fraid not, partner, and not more aspirin for you, you're bleeding too much."

Thump-thump-thump...

The unmistakable sound of an approaching chopper sent Rob's heart racing again. A feeling of excitement and relief overwhelmed him as the noise grew louder, and the ladies joined him in celebration, as they waved the chopper in.

Snap!

An unexpected sound behind them caused Tex and Rob to look questioningly at each other; instantly, they moved for a better look with the field glasses. Rob could hear someone speaking in Spanish, not too far up on the trail.

Tex lowered his glasses. "Trouble's comin' this way!"

Armand and his rebels were approaching, with weapons drawn and a wild look in their eyes, as they moved in for the kill. When they heard the chopper, they moved more quickly down the falls, hoping to reach their prey before they escaped.

"You two need to move, now!" Rob shouted at Beth Anne and Myia. "Get as close as you can to the river's edge and wait for that chopper."

Without a word of protest, the women got the message and quickly scrambled off.

Rob grabbed his weapon and ammo and looked up at Tex, who was carefully watching the trail, and taking aim up the hill with his big rifle.

"Doc, just keep an eye up yonder; they'll be in that spot there in just a minute," Tex said, pointing. "The waterfall cuts off the trail, so at least they can't flank us. I'm going up there, behind them big trees, to pick a few of 'em off. Wait for the whole nasty bunch to get out on the trail before you start firin'."

Rob nodded; "Okay. Stay low, buddy; they're coming."

Tex moved behind some cover and steadied his rifle against a tree limb, his hands never losing their shake. As the thuds of the chopper grew louder, he fired several times, the boom of his big rifle echoing down the hillside. After a short round of return fire, the first of several rebels ran onto the trail, and Rob fired his Mini-16 in short, accurate bursts. The first shots found their mark and hit the point man; Rob and Tex kept firing into the rebels, as they scrambled for cover.

A few minutes later, Tex ran down the hill and exchanged his rifle for his M-16. Both of them stayed low and sprayed the trail with a hailstorm of firepower. Bullets snapped and popped around and above them, as what was left of the patrol fired to cover their retreat.

Rob and Tex moved quickly, found the ladies and ran toward the chopper, hovering in the distance. As they got closer, they saw someone waving to them from the door, which only fueled them to run faster. "Home!" Rob said. "We're finally going home. All of us!"

Suddenly, a white streak flashed from the nearby copse of trees, and a rocket sailed right over Tex's head with a loud *swoosh* – straight at the waiting chopper.

"R.P.G.! Get down, now!" Tex yelled.

The chopper erupted into a bright ball of flame and flying debris. Its burning carcass spun downward, slamming into the riverbank, less than a hundred feet away from them. Rob managed to pull his wife and Myia down to the ground, half a second before the shockwave, shrapnel and rubble from the explosion blew over them. What was left of the chopper was engulfed in a fiery ball, so intense that they could feel the searing heat from it.

It took a moment for everyone to recover, and their ears rang, as billowing black smoke wafted overhead; everyone was shaken and disoriented from the blast.

Tex jumped to his feet, looked up into the trees and yelled: "We've gotta get out of here, now! Everyone move – downstream! Go!"

Quickly, Rob gathered himself and his gear, then guided the women through the curtain of smoke and searing heat, toward the river; Tex took up the rear, to keep an eye on the tree line.

Rob found a worn riverside trail, and they followed it along the winding river. Tex caught up with them and took point, leading the group at a faster pace. They hadn't even time to think about the horror they'd just witnessed, or the fact that they could have all been blown to bits; the group just continued their desperate run along the river, away from the rebels.

Chapter 9
THE NEWS

Back home, the news had leaked – either from the military, or from someone in Colombia; no one knew for sure who or how, but someone had put two and two together, and now everyone figured events there had something to do with the big bust. *"CARTEL BASE ATTACKED! RESCUE HELICOPTER SHOT DOWN OFF COLOMBIAN COAST!"* screamed the headlines.

Back at the station, Chief Roy was tired of the onslaught of reporters, asking questions for which he had no answers. "For the last time, I know as much as you people do at this point," he spat, angrily. "As soon as we hear anything, I will let you know." With that, he pointed at the front entrance and ordered all of them to exit his police station.

The chief, like the press, strongly suspected that the stories he had been reading in the news had something to do with Rob and Beth Anne. He had not seen or heard from Rob, even though he had stopped by his house and called him, several times, over the past few days. He thought Rob might have gone to spend time with his parents, but that seemed unlikely.

The phone rang, jolting him out of his trance.

"Chief Roy here," he answered gruffly, fearing it was yet

another media vulture. Instead, it was the F.B.I., announcing that they would be there immediately for an important meeting.

"I don't know which is worse," Roy mumbled to himself, "the feds or the press."

Just as he hung up the phone, his brother-in-law walked into his office. "Roy, there's something you should know," Bill said.

As soon as Roy had asked him to sit down, Bill then proceeded to tell the chief his own suspicions about Rob and his friend, Tex.

"Jesus, Roy, I've been hearing this on the news and seeing it on television. You think they were in that chopper that went down? We have to find out what happened; if there's any chance they made it, we can't lose them now. They went to rescue my daughter, for God's sake."

"I just found out about this mess myself, Bill," Roy confessed. "Perhaps the F.B.I. has some answers – they're on their way here now, for a meeting with me. In the meantime, try to calm down, stay positive, and – for the love of everything holy – don't say a word to those reporters."

Roy asked after his sister, and the two men talked for a while, before the phone rang again, with another call from the F.B.I.

"We'd rather meet at a hotel, on the outskirts of town," the agent on the phone said; "there's too much press at the police station."

After he hung up, Roy looked at Bill. "I'll catch up with you later," he said. "I promise I'll call as soon as we know... well, anything."

Roy took the back exit from the station, heading straight for his car and home.

There, he took a quick shower, then made a dinner of leftover meatloaf and mashed potatoes, which he gobbled up before dressing in a clean uniform. Then, with a fresh cup of coffee in hand, he left for the meeting.

He had high hopes, but he couldn't help feeling depressed. He couldn't stand the disappointment he'd heard in the children's voices; they all desperately wanted to see Rob and Beth Anne again.

As he pulled in to park at the hotel, the chief was surprised to see no one out front by the main entrance. Nevertheless, just as he had been instructed, he pulled around back and used the rear entrance.

There, two agents were posted at the door. They ignored his uniform, and insisted on checking his badge and I.D. before they would allow him in. "Go to the conference room, down the hall on the right," one of the agents said.

The nicely furnished meeting room was buzzing with activity, and Roy quickly spotted Agent Sanders, sitting with a group of important-looking people, which included military officers. Roy sat next to her at the big table, and opened his briefcase.

Agent Sanders got up and walked to the podium, where she thanked everyone for coming at short notice, then got right down to business. "You've all seen the headlines, so let's just get to what we have. First, we know Officer Marrino was involved in the arrest of a key member of a well-known Colombian drug cartel; during the bust, one of the suspects was killed and another taken into custody, and a large quantity of pure cocaine was seized. Our sources in Colombia have confirmed that the cartel took Officer Marrino's wife hostage, as a bartering chip for the release of their man in prison. Unfortunately, we also know that it is difficult to deal with drug smugglers and terrorists."

After another sip of her coffee, Agent Sanders began covering her ass: "We had no idea that Officer Marrino would try to free them by force. Our intel indicates that he was in contact with an individual from Texas, and that the two flew to Bogotá, Colombia, a few days before the incident. Chief Roy, is there any light you can shed on this situation?"

Roy looked around at the unfamiliar faces. "I know Rob loves his family, and he's the kind of man who would risk everything for them. He was distressed, but he said nothing to me about any such plans; he only told me that he needed some time off, to get his kids settled and clear his head."

Suddenly, one of the suits stood up and began to speak: "Ladies and gentlemen, I am Director Stanley Hopper of the C.I.A., special adjutant to the presidential cabinet on military affairs."

The room grew quiet, and all eyes were instantly on Director Hopper.

"I hope I don't have to remind you that all matters discussed here are to be kept strictly confidential. I have the backing of the highest authority, and the president of the United States has taken a personal interest in this matter; our country is, and has been for many years, working alongside the Colombian government to break up these heinous drug cartels and their operations. I think it's best to hand the technical matters over to my friend and colleague, General Samuel Jaskins, of U.S. Army Special Forces."

The general, a tall, middle-aged African-American man, walked around the table as he spoke. "First, I want to thank everyone for their cooperation, in this delicate situation we now find ourselves in. In our research and investigation, we have left no stone unturned. We know that Officer Robert Marrino is a highly decorated veteran of the Vietnam War, an Army combat medic, and a silent hero of the highest order; he was known by his brothers-in-arms as 'Doc'. The individual from Texas is one of those old war buddies: a sergeant with the First Marines. His real name is Richard Larson, but he goes, quite fittingly, by the name 'Tex'. He is the best of the best: a legendary sniper with amazing capability. Both men served together in the jungles of Vietnam. As for this current unauthorized mission of theirs, we know that they made their arrangements through a military contact, and they also had help executing their insertion."

The room remained silent, as Jaskins sipped his water, then continued: "The truth is, we don't know exactly where they are, or if they escaped with any captives. Our surveillance has revealed that the cartel camp is in shambles – presumably, if a team of two have managed to wreak that much havoc whilst still freeing the captives, that is even more proof of their courage and skill.

"We know that the chopper intending to pick them up was destroyed; what we don't know is whether or not they were on that helicopter when it exploded – this, ladies and gentlemen, is what the president wants and needs to find out. In fact, now that the story has leaked, *everyone* wants to know. I have been instructed to gather all relevant information from our contacts in Colombia, and from our intelligence here.

"As we speak, a team is setting up for insertion. We will neutralize any remaining cartel forces which stand in our way, then sweep the area for survivors; one way or another, we *will* bring them home... all of them. Our line of communication will go through normal channels, and Special Agent Sanders and her team will be kept in the loop. If anyone learns any useful information, or has a question, please feel free to contact me."

While questions sprung up around the table, Agent Sanders sat in quiet thought. She couldn't help feeling responsible, for she knew that she'd had a big hand in the matter – the hand which presently held a file folder, full of the confidential information which had helped set the mission into motion in the first place. Now, she could only cling to her hope that they were still alive. *At least, now the word is out, they're getting help,* she thought, trying to find some bright spot in all of it.

The meeting adjourned within the hour, and everyone quickly dispersed; they all had someone to meet or call, or somewhere to be; the military was already on their way to Colombia.

Roy did his best to thank everyone for their help and concern, then left to pay Bill and Susan a visit. He was happy to be sharing the good news that help was on its way to Rob and Beth Anne; he only hoped that it wasn't too little, too late.

Chapter 10
THE RUN

Back in the jungle, the group moved downstream as quickly as possible, with Tex on point, the women in the middle and Rob bringing up the rear. Everyone was loaded down with gear, but no one said a word; they were still trying to recover from the shocking scene which had unfolded at the river's edge, and trying to cope with the fact that they'd almost lost their lives. No more choppers; they were now on their own, and on the run in Colombia.

The remnants of the trail ended, and they were forced to slow down. Tex checked the compass settings and Rob looked for a way through the heavy growth. It was rough going, hacking through the thick brush and thorny foliage, but it also made for good cover, for which they were thankful – especially when they heard muffled explosions in the distance. They looked up at the sky, watching the black smoke drifting over the treetops, reminding them that their rescue ride was still burning.

Grateful that Tex had found a narrow trail, which made their trek a little easier, Rob made his way up from the rear. "I've been scanning our flank; it doesn't look like we're being tailed – at least, not yet."

Tex smiled. "Hmm, that's odd. Maybe the rebels think

we were on board that bird when it went down. They are going to check the area though, so we've gotta keep moving."

After another mile or so, they finally stopped to rest under some large trees, a reasonably safe distance from the base. Everyone's clothes were filthy and soaked with sweat. While the others shared water and rested for a moment, Tex carefully set up a tripwire, linking it to a claymore on the trail behind them.

"This oughta be a nice little surprise for our rebel friends," he said, with an ornery smile. "Just watch out for it if we end up comin' back this way. If nothing else, it'll be a good sign to warn us they're coming our way. Like you said, Rob, it seems that they've pulled back for now, but I'm sure they'll come after us again, when they examine the wreckage and don't find any of us in it."

"Well, where do we go from here?" Rob asked.

"That's a good question," Tex said. "I did manage to grab this baby back there – maybe it can still help us call in the cavalry."

Rob grinned, when he saw that Tex was holding the transponder. "That was quick thinking, Tex. I don't know how you managed to snatch it, but I'm sure glad you did; it may well get us a ride out of here."

Myia stood up, suddenly. "I know place, not far. My people... they help us." She pointed to a place on the map, then gestured downstream, to the north.

While Tex and Myia discussed the plan, Rob checked on

Beth Anne. He was pleased to find that she looked much better: not so pale and frail, and her fever was all but gone. "How do you feel?" he asked.

"Tired, but okay. I don't know what happened; I just felt... so sick. Rob, I'm so sorry for those men in the chopper; they risked their lives to come here for us, and they never stood a chance. I'm scared, Rob: that cartel is evil; they'll kill us all, the first chance they get. How are we ever going to get back home?"

Rob did his best to comfort her. "Beth Anne, we'll get out of this, one way or another," he promised, holding her close and stroking her hair. "We were so close to being free back there. I know it didn't work out the way we planned, but let's try to think positive and keep hope alive; we can't ever give up. And, you've got the best men on the job; if there's a way out, Tex and I will find it!"

They drank water and ate energy bars, before resuming their journey – this time, toward Myia's hometown.

"We're covering a lot of ground," Tex said, sounding impressed. "We keep going at this clip, we might just make it by nightfall."

As they continued their long hike through the jungle, they saw locals, fishing on the other side of the stream, as they turned north. Myia said they needed to be careful, as there were hordes of cartel spies lurking all around the area. The dense, thick jungle once again reminded Rob of Vietnam, another place where he had always been on the lookout for enemies.

Even as surefooted as Rob and Tex were, it was not easy for any of them to maintain an even pace, through the overgrown cover and sloping, uneven terrain. To complicate the conditions even more, nasty, biting flies were driving them all crazy. Rob shared his repellant, but it did little to help against the bugs' attack.

The ladies seemed to be holding up remarkably well, but Rob was worried about Tex, whose wound was still bleeding profusely. He feared Tex's pain and blood loss would soon wear him down, but the war hero didn't complain; he just pushed on, like a machine, leading them forward – that was just his way.

It was steamy and hot, and they walked on and on, for what seemed like forever, perspiring from the humidity and itching from the bug bites.

"Hold up, Tex," Rob finally said, out of breath; "we need to take a break and drink some water. Also, I wanna take a look at those bandages again."

Tex looked down, only now realizing that the blood had soaked through them and was again running down his arm. "Might not be a bad idea, Doc," he said. He led them to a small clearing, where they could rest by the cool water of the small, fast flowing stream.

Rob plopped down next to his buddy and started to change his bandages. "Listen pal, I need you to keep this arm as still as possible," he ordered, as he fashioned a makeshift sling out of the remainder of the bandages.

Tex grimaced; "Hmm, that means I only got one good

arm to shoot with, Doc."

"Well, if you don't keep this one still, I'll shoot you myself," Rob threatened, teasingly.

"My town not far now," Myia said, walking over to them. "We move away from river." She pointed upward, to a ridge on the hillside to the east, which looked to be a few miles away.

"Can we trust them, these people of yours?" Tex asked.

"Yes, yes," Myia said, nodding her head. "All love my family; loyal to us. Father will be at ranch, unless he is looking for me."

"A ranch, huh? Well, now you're speakin' my language, lady!" Tex said, with a charming smile and a wink.

They talked it over for a while and the ladies decided to cool off in the stream. Rob and Tex joined in and the splashing and joking began. It felt good to laugh, it helped ease the tension. The plan was to sneak around the town and straight onto the ranch grounds; they all agreed that the fewer the number of eyes which fell on them, the better. The last thing they needed was a run-in with any enemy spies.

*

Back at the crash site, Armand and the rebels were scouring the wreckage, hoping to find bodies among the debris.

Armand had foolishly walked right by the transponder case, without spotting it. Then, like a dog on the hunt, he bent closer to the ground and followed the river.

"Did you see them board the 'copter before you fired?" he demanded, yelling at the man who fired the R.P.G. launcher.

The rebel shrugged, and his eyes grew wide with fear, as he admitted: "I am not sure, sir."

"Of course not!" Armand barked. He then pointed along the river. "They went this way, you idiot! Go and find them," he ordered, sending ten of his best men out as a search party.

*

Rob and the group followed a small, worn footpath to the top of the ridge. From there, they could see the edge of town, just ahead, obvious by its red-tiled rooftops, looming just above the tree line.

Tex lowered his field glasses, but before he could say anything, a muffled explosion echoed up from the river.

"Whoa," Rob muttered.

Tex smiled. "Ah-ha! I was wondering when our friends would find my little present. That oughta hold 'em off for a while! Still, they'll be coming; c'mon, we gotta move out."

"There's no time to waste; we're killin' daylight here," Rob added.

After carefully moving their way around the little village, they finally found the side-road Myia was looking for, although it wasn't much of a road at all; rather, a narrow, winding line of crumbling asphalt and sand, which led out of town. They stayed off to the side of the road, until they were about a quarter-mile past the city.

"There! We go this way," Myia announced, as they reached a small field bordered with wire fencing.

They turned away from the road, then stopped on the soft, green grass to rest in the shade and replenish their fluids. As always, Tex took the opportunity to scan the area ahead. "Looks pretty clear and quiet to me, y'all," he said.

They started again, along a narrow path through the cover, until they came upon a large clearing: a grass field, bordered by white-picket fences.

"Now we go to house," Myia said, pointing.

They were all relieved, as they looked at the ranch spread out before them; everyone was eager to get out of the unforgiving bush, and into more comfortable surroundings. The large, stone ranch-house and stables were on the other side of the field; several black and brown bay horses were feeding in the pasture.

Tex smiled. "Those are some fine-looking animals, ma'am," he said.

Rob added: "Like she said, Tex, her father is a very important man."

They followed the fence line until they came to a locked gate. There, they decided to wait for the cover of darkness, before they risked crossing the large open field. It seemed to take forever for the light to give way to the shadows of night.

Finally, Rob stood up; "It's go time."

They grabbed their gear and got ready. Before hopping the fence, Tex set up the transponder, and Rob helped him attach it to one of the posts. Finally, with the last of them over the fence, they ran into the grassy field with Myia in the lead.

They noticed lights coming on around the house, as they moved toward the ranch in the distance.

Chapter 11
CALL TO ARMS

Back in the States, planning for the rescue mission was continuing.

General Jaskins was elated by the good news from Director Hopper; he was also impressed that the man was able to speak directly to the president on the telephone. As soon as he had all the details, he arranged with his staff to get the word out to all concerned, and booked an immediate flight to the new command center, for the coming operation in Colombia.

Within five hours, Jaskins had arrived at the Florida Air Force base, as directed. The long flight had left him fatigued, but he was eager to get underway. He immediately found the officers' club, made a few phone calls and gulped down some coffee with his lunch, hoping that the caffeine would help him recover from his jetlag in a hurry. Within the hour, his escort arrived and he departed, on his way to meet with the other V.I.P.s on the mission.

On the way, he couldn't stop thinking about the president's last words to him: "General, I want our people home. I have already contacted the Colombian president, and we have his full support in this matter. I want this done quickly; please do whatever is necessary to get them out of there. The cartels have been thorns in our side for too long; now it's time for the American people to see the justice that we deserve." It was unbelievable to Jaskins that he had been given full authority by the commander-in-chief himself! Truly, it was what he had prepared for all his life – and now that power was in his grasp.

With power comes responsibility, he reminded himself. He knew that he had to plan carefully, that he had to choose the very best people for the job, and there was absolutely no room for error. *It's in my hands, and the lives of everyone involved are at stake.*

As they drove across the busy airbase, Jaskins looked at the large, brick and steel building ahead of them. The car pulled through a checkpoint, and his driver let him out in front of the central command center.

Base Commander Harold Simson was there to greet Jaskins at the front entrance; he introduced himself and his staff. Jaskins was glad to be reuniting with some old friends, with whom he had served during his tour in Vietnam.

They walked into a large, well-furnished conference room, where Jaskins looked around him at more officers; men and women representing every military branch. He poured himself a hot cup of black coffee, grabbed a donut from the serving table, and sat down at the huge oak table.

Air Force Commander Simson called the meeting to order, and it was surprisingly quiet within moments, the only noise the clicking of briefcase locks opening, and the shuffling of paperwork.

"Ladies and gentlemen, I have the good news we've all been waiting and hoping for: our contacts in Colombia have picked up a signal from a standard, U.S. Army-issued transponder; the location is just inland from the northern coast of Colombia – about four miles northeast of the cartel base. Our group did not make it into their chopper – thank God; there's good intel that they managed to escape to another area."

The quiet in the room was broken by several heavy sighs of relief.

"As we all know," Simson continued, "the president and his administration have taken a personal interest in this situation; he is especially eager to get our people home. We all have a big job ahead of us, but please know that all the resources of the U.S. Air Force are at your disposal.

"Now my colleague, General Jaskins, will provide his initial briefing on the recovery operation."

Jaskins walked up, shook hands with Commander Simson, then stood next to a detailed wall map. He drew circles on the map with a thick, black marker, indicating the locations of the cartel base, the transponder signal and the surrounding area.

"First, I want to thank everyone for coming at such short notice; second, I am delighted to hear that we now have a viable location on our people.

"As the commander said, we have a big job to do, and not much time to do it. Considering the circumstances and the limited timeframe, this must be a carefully coordinated mission. I have already conferred with some of you by phone, and I've been diligently researching our options; I believe I've come up with a workable plan. But, if anyone has anything helpful to add, now is the time for us to discuss it."

The room remained quiet, all eyes still on the map.

The general took another sip of coffee, stifled a yawn left over from his long flight, then pointed to another area on the map. "'Operation Sledgehammer' will consist of three parts. First, an Army Rangers team will execute insertion at this location here," he pointed, "just south of the transponder signal; their mission is to find our people as quickly as possible and secure the area for extraction. Next, we will time a precision Air Force strike, moving from the coast into this area here," he pointed again, "where the chopper went down. They will create a diversion and completely destroy any remaining cartel assets, including the terrorist rebels we suspect are involved; heavy firepower will be necessary to minimize this threat. Finally, when the Rangers alert us that it's a go, the third phase will involve extraction by U.S. Naval forces. Their mission is simple: to move in and get everyone out. Stealth, timing and precision are of the utmost importance, in every phase of this mission."

With that said, General Jaskins resumed his seat and began thumbing through his paperwork.

Several around the table offered suggestions and asked questions, and endless discussion of the details ensued.

Several pots of coffee were consumed, and a dinner buffet fueled them for conversations which would carry on well into the night; the hours waned, as every detail was ironed out.

Finally, calls were made, orders were given, and wheels were set in motion to accomplish the extraction. As always, it would be up to the troops in uniform – the boots on the ground – to venture into harm's way and get the job done.

Chapter 12
REUNION

At the ranch, the escapees hustled across the open field and circled around to the rear of the large ranch house. Myia went in first, slipping into the servants' back door. While the others waited, Tex clicked off the safety on his sidearm, just in case.

After some commotion, Myia came to the doorway and waved them inside, with a broad smile on her face. "Come! Please! My family waiting," she invited.

They followed her into a large kitchen, where a short, dark-haired man rushed over to greet them. With a smile as wide as Myia's, he shook Rob's hand and nodded his thanks. At the same time, Myia's mother embraced Beth Anne in a warm, friendly hug, muttering her own words of appreciation.

"I am Eduardo," Myia's father announced, in English as clear as his daughter's. "God bless you! You bring our Myia home."

Myia went on to introduce the rest of the family: her mother, Maria, and Antonio, her little brother. All of them thanked Rob and Tex, over and over again, in both Spanish and English, for saving Myia from the cartel.

"We were so worried; she was missing three days," Maria

said, with tears in her eyes, as she lovingly petted her daughter's dark hair. "We thought..." She was unable to finish the sentence, for all of her sobbing.

Eduardo continued: "We pray for her. The cartel – those animals – take her; they want to steal my land. I take care of you all; please come. Let us eat and we talk."

The rustic home was enormous, framed with wooden beams; it reminded Tex of his place back home. A brownstone fireplace was the centerpiece of the living room.

Once they were all comfortably seated there, Myia came over and handed Beth Anne some fresh clothes. "Come," she then said, escorting the group to a pair of guest bedrooms, sharing a large bathroom between them. Tex graciously took the smaller of the two rooms, and they all stashed their packs and freshened up, before returning to the kitchen.

Maria carried a steaming pot to the table, as the servants brought freshly-baked bread, wine and side dishes. The food was hot and a touch too spicy, but very good.

As Rob and Tex talked about their adventure, Eduardo couldn't believe they had made it out of the base alive. He couldn't thank them enough for hitting getting his girl free. "I have fought them many times," he said; "many good people have died. I hate them."

Tex smiled, as he looked at Eduardo; "Well, last night the cartel got a taste of their own medicine."

Everyone joined in the conversation, and it was good to

relax, dine and laugh. There were smiles all around, and the women looked so much better than they had just a day earlier.

After dinner, Eduardo asked Rob and Tex to join him in his office. He introduced them to the two armed guards posted by his desk, whom he then dismissed, with orders to wait outside the door. Once they were alone, he said: "I call doctor. He is Myia's uncle; lives just down street. We trust him."

"I'm glad to hear it," Rob said, as he took a seat in one of the soft leather chairs. "I could use a little help treating that wound of Tex's."

"Pssh; it's just a scratch," Tex argued, at which Rob rolled his eyes.

"Here, for you," Eduardo said, shoving a black, leather-bound packet across the desk, toward them.

Scrunching up his brow in confusion, Tex opened it. "Whoa," he uttered; it was full of cash. "Uh, thanks Eduardo, but we didn't come for money. Right now, we just need a safe place to stay, 'til our ride shows up to take us home."

Eduardo lit a thick Cuban cigar and continued: "My friends, this is gift, for the life of my child. I was to ready to give everything to cartel; now, the money is yours. But, do not tell anyone; it is our secret."

Tex laid the pack down on the desk, gesturing for Rob to join him in the far corner. "We have to accept it, Rob," he said; "if we don't, he'll be offended."

"I don't care about the money; I just want us to all get out of here in one piece," Rob replied.

Tex returned to the desk, shook Eduardo's hand, and picked up the packet again. "Thank you, my good man. It isn't necessary, but it is surely appreciated, and will be put to good use."

Rob stepped forward and shook hands with Eduardo. "Thank you, sir, thanks for helping us out."

Eduardo smiled, then filled glasses with brandy for each of them. "Now, let us talk of plan. I have family in many parts of country; many interests: I own houses, horses and coffee – but, most important is land. My friends will watch cartel; you will be safe here for now. Rest and enjoy." With that, he offered a cigar to each of them, and handed them their brandy.

Rob took a long, slow pull of the sweet, warm liquid, before he told Eduardo about the transponder, assuring him: "God willing, help is probably already on the way."

The men sat drinking and smoking, talking over the details for well over an hour. Then, they returned to the kitchen, where they found the ladies still sitting at the table, chatting with Maria.

Eduardo motioned to the servants; "Please, some wine and dessert for our guests."

They gathered around the oak dining table, sipping on light, sweet wine and enjoying lighthearted conversation.

For the time being, the plan was very simple: they would get some rest and wait to see if anyone picked up the transponder signal. Eduardo expected that cartel spies would be snooping around, looking for Myia; as a precaution, he posted several of his ranch hands and guards, to serve as lookouts around the ranch perimeter. He suggested that Rob and Tex stow their weapons and gear next to their bedroom doors, so that, when help came, they would be ready to go.

The doctor arrived as planned, and was greeted at the door by Eduardo and his family. Myia's uncle was very happy to see her, and she was excited to introduce him to her new friends. "This is my uncle, Alex," she said.

Alex, dressed in an immaculate, white linen suit, removed his matching white, black-banded hat, set down his medical pack and shook Rob's hand. When the big man offered his hand for a shake, Alex noticed Tex's bandages. "Ah! I see. How is arm?"

Tex winced in pain, as Alex touched his bandages. "It's starting to throb some, Doctor."

"Come with me," Alex said.

Rob and Tex followed him into the bedroom.

"There," the doctor said, pointing to the bed.

As Tex lay down, Rob moved a lamp closer to them. "It's been bleeding pretty badly," he said to Alex. He then went on to fill the doctor in on how Tex had been injured.

Alex moved a chair to the bedside and opened up his med-pack. He cut away the bandages and carefully examined the gaping hole, then smiled at Rob. "Well, you do well – help keep clean – but we must open; clean out. Help me?"

"Of course," Rob said.

Tex's eyes grew wide. "Hold up. If you two are gonna do some excavatin' in there, I might need a couple more bottles of that wine," he said, with a grin.

"Oh, hush, you big baby," Rob chided; "we both know you've been through worse."

"You feel nothing," Alex reassured him, pulling a large syringe from his bag. He gave Tex an injection and, in less than a minute, the big man was out like a light.

The surgery took about an hour. Alex and Rob did a fine job of cleaning and removing the small fragments of shrapnel and cloth, which had embedded deep in Tex's bicep. When the stitches were done, Alex inserted another syringe into Tex's shoulder – a dose of penicillin to prevent infection – and Rob handled the redressing of the wound with fresh bandages.

Before leaving, Alex said: "I happy to help; you bring our Myia home! Wound will heal, as long as he takes pills, keep clean, rests..." A somber look suddenly came over his face, as he warned: "People talk; say cartel looking for you."

"I'm sure they are," Rob said, "but hopefully we'll be gone before they find us."

After Alex had left, Tex stirred; a silly smile crossed his face. "The arm feels better already, Doc."

"Right, man," Rob replied. "You need to keep it still and rest a while, and you'll be good as new."

"But, it's my shootin'—" Tex could not finish; he was out cold again, the moment his head fell back against the pillow.

Rob found Beth Anne fast asleep in the next bedroom, and he gently slipped under the covers, behind her. It was such a warm, wonderful feeling to be so close to her; to smell her hair again. *She looks like an angel,* he thought. Silently, he prayed: *Lord, please give me the strength to keep her safe; to make it out of this nightmare.* He vowed that no one would ever take her from him again.

Soon, he drifted off, into sweet dreams of his children, and all of them being home together – a dream which still seemed so far, far away.

Chapter 13
FIRE IN THE NIGHT

Around midnight, Beth Anne jerked Rob awake. "Rob! Rob! Get up!"

"Huh? What is it?" he stuttered, confused, as he looked into her troubled eyes.

She turned on the light. "I-I think I heard gunshots, and—"

Blam!

Rob instantly jumped out of bed. "There's a problem out in the field," he said, as the second shot rang out.

"Where are you going?" she asked, panicking.

"Honey, please calm down. Just stay in the house and keep low, away from the windows," he said. "I'll check it out."

As soon as Rob flung the door open, he found Tex standing on the other side of it, his arms full of gear and weapons.

"Well, Doc, it sounds like we're in for some action again, my friend," he said, using his good arm to hand Rob his rifle and sidearm.

Rob had a wild look in his eyes, his hands beginning to shake as he grabbed his weapons. "This time, it's my turn to be the trigger man," Rob said. "I'll kill them all! It's my life for her!"

Quickly, they dressed and headed for the kitchen, as another round of shots rang out. Tex looked out of the kitchen window, to see bright flashes out near the fence line.

Beth Anne and Myia rushed into the kitchen, and Beth Anne grabbed Rob's hand. "Why do you have to go out there? Please, stay here with us," she said, with that scared, helpless look in her eyes again – a look which broke Rob's heart.

Rob did his best to calm his wife down. "Babe, it's going to be fine. Please, just stay in the house; lock the doors, stay down and stay away from the windows. Tex and I are just gonna take a quick look around."

Eduardo hurried in, wearing a holster on his belt and carrying a double-barrel shotgun. He opened a cabinet door and retrieved an oversize silver revolver and some ammo, then handed the shotgun to one of his guards. "Stay with women," Eduardo ordered.

He then approached Rob and Tex, with another of his trusted guards in tow, and pulled out his enormous pistol. "Cartel animals have come for us," he said.

Tex replied: "Looks like all the action's out on that fence line; Eduardo, your men need our help. We'd better get out there and put a stop to it, 'fore those animals bust in here. Let's go!"

Before they left, Rob gave Beth Anne a hug. "Just remember to stay down, out of sight. And don't go outside, no matter what."

"We promise to stay low and wait until you come back, Rob," she answered, sadly.

Rob smiled. "You can count on it."

Outside, Tex, Rob and the guard followed Eduardo around the side of the house. Rob and Tex moved toward the fence, where they noticed two of the guards were pointing at them, from a cluster of trees just beyond the fence; Eduardo and his men crawled behind the watering troughs, to provide cover fire. Rob and Tex crouched for a moment, before running toward a large tree at the edge of the field.

When shots rang out overhead, and they saw muzzle flashes, Tex yelled in response: "Open fire!"

A hail of gunfire instantly rang out, as a shower of bullets rained into the trees.

Rob suddenly caught something out of the corner of his eye: a dark figure, moving nearby. He drew his rifle on the target but, just as he pulled the trigger, he saw a bright flash. "R.P.G.!" he yelled, instinctively dropping to the ground.

The rocket streaked over them, exploding when it struck a tree limb. Debris flew all over; jolted by the shockwave of the blast, they were left covered in twigs and rubble, and feeling more than a little shaken.

When Rob was finally able to move into firing position, he swung his rifle around, emptying his clip into the rebels moving along the cover; Tex fired his handgun and hit two, as they tried to climb over the fence.

"Grenade!" Rob yelled, just before stepping out from

cover and lobbing one, then another, over the fence and into the trees. The powerful blasts lit up the fence line with red-hot shrapnel.

Rob then signaled for everyone to hold their fire. They watched and waited. When there was no return fire, Rob and Tex moved in for a closer look. On the other side of the fence, bodies were strewn here and there; the terrorists had pulled back in a hurry, leaving three of their dead behind.

Rob smiled. "It looks like we got the better of them – for now."

"Yeah, I don't think they'll be back tonight," Tex said.

"I still don't like it, Tex; what about the ones who got away? We need to get out of here, quickly."

"Roger that, partner," Tex agreed; "I don't like it either. I got a feeling they'll bring reinforcements next time. We better pray someone picks up that signal."

Rob, with one of the guards, checked along the fence line and searched the dead rebels, stripping the bodies of any weapons and ammo.

*

The survivors among the rebel search party gathered what gear was left and fled back to the river's edge in a panic, where they radioed Armand to explain what had happened.

"What?! Three dead?" Armand yelled out, "They will pay for the lives of my people! We know where they are, and they will pay! Sit tight for now and let me know if you see anything; I need time to gather weapons and more men. I will meet you on the trail at first light."

*

Back at the ranch, Tex and Rob made their way back to the water troughs and were happy to see Eduardo and his men were okay.

"Come, let us go inside," Eduardo said. "We get sleep. Be ready; maybe cartel tomorrow."

In the kitchen, the women looked clearly frightened, but they were relieved to see that everyone was okay. Rob took a quick look at Tex's arm: it seemed okay, and it had stopped bleeding.

"Trouble is over for now," Eduardo assured his wife and daughter. He then went into his office, to talk to his men and set up watch for the rest of the night. He called in some extra reinforcements of his own: friends he knew from the area.

Rob and Tex sat with Beth Anne for a while, trying to unwind, and they discussed their options for getting back home. Myia and Maria flittered about the kitchen, killing time and nervous energy by whipping up snacks for their guests.

Eduardo returned from his office, with a bottle in his hand. "Friends, you will drink with me?" he invited.

Maria served bread and cheese, and they enjoyed more of Eduardo's fine fruity brandy; Tex asked for black coffee, instead.

"I'll bunk outside, with the guards," he added.

Rob knew that there was no arguing with him – besides, everyone felt a little safer with Tex out there on guard, in his element. "Thanks, Tex," he simply said.

Tex nodded, then grabbed his pack with his good arm, taking the mug of coffee from Myia with the other. "Thank ya, ma'am," he said, before slipping out into the darkness.

The brandy did its job and, before long, they were all ready to try for some sleep. Rob put his loaded rifle and sidearm next to the bed, before turning out the light. He snuggled close to Beth Anne and prayed, again, for a safe journey home.

Out by the guardhouse, Tex lit up a Marlboro and stared out into the dark landscape, scanning the area with his night-vision headset. Everything seemed to be quiet – he hoped it would stay that way.

*

Back near the cartel's base, though, things were not quiet at all. Armand and his rebels were scrambling around, amassing more men for one final attack on the ranch. Every available rebel, along with as much weaponry and ammo as they could carry, were loaded into their truck.

"I will avenge my brother and my lost men at any cost!" Armand screamed, before barking more orders at his men.

Chapter 14
SLEDGEHAMMER

Within twenty-four hours of receiving the transponder signal, a U.S. Army C-140 transport lifted off, and a Navy carrier task force moved into position, about 250 miles off the north Colombian coast.

At the airbase, General Jaskins and his team watched the plane as it banked, then took off into the horizon, at a southeast heading. Silently, Jaskins prayed for their success. He knew that they had all done their due diligence, to be thorough in the planning stages, and now the wheels were set in motion; it was, as always, up to the troops to venture into harm's way and get the job done.

On the transport, the troops were unusually calm and quiet. A few commented about the mission now and then but, for the most part, the only noise was the constant drumming of the jet engines. As the sixteen heavily-armed Army rangers methodically checked their gear, weapons, and ammo, all understood the importance of the mission, and all were clear on the details of what they were supposed to do. Even more importantly, every man was focused and determined to do it right.

Three hours later, the big plane banked and slowly started to descend. The rangers checked their chutes and set up the line for the drop. If everything went as planned, they would insert about two miles south of the transponder signal.

Out at sea, Admiral Sinclair stood on the bridge, watching, as his mighty ship turned into the wind. He glanced toward the sky, as four Air Force F-15 attack jets launched from the carrier in quick succession; the admiral gave his crew a thumbs-up, as the jets thundered into the horizon. He was confident in his men, and he was certain the mission would prove successful.

Within thirty minutes, the jets were on their final approach to the target, moving toward land in a staggered formation. They flew low and fast over the water, heading straight for the cartel base.

"Com One, this is Tango Six. Copy?" said the squadron leader, breaking the radio silence. "We've got a radar lock for target."

"Roger, Tango Six; it's a go for 'Sledgehammer'."

The other pilots followed Tango 6 in tight formation, the attack jets sweeping over the coastline and soaring over the outer guard station.

*

The rebel guards looked up in awe, as the powerful jets screamed past them. One guard reached for his radio, but was interrupted from calling for help, when he noticed a dark shape spiraling toward them. Everything went black before he finished keying his mic.

Just like that, it was too late, and there was no one to warn the rebels, who were rebuilding the camp. It was also too late to hide the trucks of cocaine and heroin.

One by one, the jets streaked over the base, releasing an awesome barrage of bombs and missiles. What remained of the base and surrounding area was blown to pieces in a matter of minutes. Thick, black smoke and flames filled the sky, as the mighty jets banked hard, then accelerated back out over the water.

Armand, still on the trail with his two trucks of rebels, was only a mile or so from the blasts – he screamed and cursed when he heard the noise. He told everyone to stop and get out of the trucks, barking: "Go! Go! See if anyone has survived."

One of his drivers and two rebel guards jumped into one of the trucks and took off toward the base.

*

Back at the ranch, Rob was jerked awake in the wee hours, by an odd sound and sensation. He dashed over to the window and peered out, but saw nothing out of the ordinary in the breaking dawn.

Then, just as he was putting on his shoes, so he could head outside for a better look, another explosion blasted his ears. He looked out of the front door and saw bright flashes on the horizon, coming from the direction of the base.

It took a moment for his brain to wake up, but he quickly realized it had to be an air or ground attack on the cartel. "They came after all," he muttered to himself. He ran outside and, in his excitement, almost knocked Tex over.

Tex smiled, as he watched the fireballs expanding in the distance. "Doc, the cavalry's ridin' in; they musta heard our signal. We better get our butts movin', before we miss our flight!"

The whole family was up now, looking out of the windows, yet Beth Anne was, surprisingly, still snoring in bed when Rob nudged her. "Hey girl, let's go. Help is on the way."

She jumped awake. "What? Who? Do you think they'll find us?"

"Tex and I think its Army, or maybe Air Force – they've attacked the cartel base. If they got a lock on our signal, they'll locate us with no problem."

She was so excited she started to put her pants on backwards, not bothering to tie her shoes. Rob laughed at her as she struggled to get dressed. He grabbed his gear, and the two of them headed down to the kitchen, to see what the others were up to. Myia and her parents were looking out of the windows, while Tex was stood at the door, watching the fence line with his field glasses.

"You will leave us soon," Eduardo said. He picked up the leather packet, which was lying on the table, and handed it to Rob. "Please no forget your things, my friends. We never forget what you do for our Myia."

The ladies hugged, while Rob and Tex again thanked Eduardo and Maria for their kindness, and his generous gift; Rob quickly stuffed the cash into the bottom of his backpack.

Tex returned to scanning the fence line, and they all watched and waited. "Shouldn't take 'em long, if they got a lock on our signal," he said.

Now near full daylight, they slipped outside for a good look around. Then, with Tex on point, they moved, single file, across the field and away from the house. The transponder was out by the fence where they first came in, so they decided it would be best to wait there.

When they reached the transponder, they saw that the little green light was still blinking. "Thank God it's still working, Tex. I was worried the rebels would find it," Rob said.

Tex smiled. "I figure if help comes they'll come up from the river, the way we did. We won't know if they're friend or foe, so we need to be careful."

"Roger that, Tex; maybe it's a small Special Forces team. We don't have a radio, but I'm sure they'll set off some smoke or a flare, when they get close."

Tex smiled again. "I see you've not forgotten the tactics we learned all them years ago. Once we've confirmed that they're the good guys, we can signal them with this smoke grenade, and wave our white flag."

Beth Anne came over, carrying Rob's med-pack. "Let's have a look at that wound, big boy," she said, with a wink.

Knowing he had no choice in the matter, Tex just bit his lip, as she changed his bandages and gave him another dose of his pills.

"The stitches look good and the swelling is down," she diagnosed. "I think you're going to survive."

"Let's hope so," Tex said; "I got horses to feed."

"I hope you can still shoot straight, big guy," Rob teased.

Tex smiled and picked up his trusty sniper rifle, with his good arm; "Just put one of those cartel rebels on target, and I'll show you, real quick."

"Listen, Tex, you should take it easy; we don't want those stitches opening up on you."

"Yeah, well, all we can do right now is watch and wait, huh?" Tex said, staring off into the distance.

Rob looked at his friend, holding the rifle, and again his mind flashed back to those times of war. He remembered the watching and waiting – and all the other unknowns. It started to wear on his nerves, and his hands started shaking again. He was doing his best to hold on to his hope, and to calm down, as he prayed once more for a safe ride back home.

Chapter 15
SILENT STRIKE

On the drop plane, the sixteen men waited patiently for their jump instructions.

General Jaskins had handpicked each man himself. They were the elite of the elite; an experienced team, committed and determined to performing a successful mission. There was no small-talk and no joking around; all were deep in thought, contemplating what they were about to do.

When the call came from H.Q., confirming the final go-ahead, the plane dropped more altitude and turned inland. As it dropped below the cloud cover, the jumpers formed a line; they could all see the smoke and flames, billowing from the cartel base to the west of them. At the predetermined location, the flight crew opened the bay doors and the green light came on above their heads. Then, one by one, the rangers jumped out, into the early-dawn sky.

Sixteen opened parachutes wafted toward the target area, hoping to end up in a field, beside a river. Team leader Lieutenant Abrams was one of the first to touch ground, and he immediately dutifully kept watch for any stray chutes; gratefully, everyone landed close by.

The team stripped out of their jump gear and

immediately began to bury their chutes. Then, after a quick headcount, Abrams reviewed his compass headings and map.

With quick precision, the rangers checked their weapons, formed up and moved out, for the run toward the target area. They moved swiftly and silently, through the thick jungle, slowing the pace as they neared the river. The bright-red sun was just starting to rise over the horizon, as the rangers moved along the riverbank with deadly determination. They were dressed in full camouflage, their faces painted black and green; they easily blended in with their surroundings, almost invisible to the naked eye. Abrams checked his map and compass headings again, then led the team away from the river and uphill, along an overgrown trail.

Lieutenant Abrams, a war veteran himself, was the only one amongst them who had served in Vietnam. For him, this was more than just another mission for his country; his fellow 'Nam veterans needed help, and he had no intention of leaving any man or woman behind.

Abrams signaled to hold: he had noticed something ahead of them, alongside the trail. When they moved closer, Abrams realized he was looking at three dead bodies – at least, what was left of them. He immediately noted that they were all in uniform: F.A.R.C. rebels, for sure. It was such a gruesome scene that one of the rangers actually vomited, overcome by the gore of blood and guts.

Abrams searched the surrounding area. He crouched

down and picked up a piece of wire and a metal fragment. "Looks like someone set a claymore – it's gotta be our boys," he said, with a smile. "They're still on the run; hopefully, they're still alive!"

They continued with renewed energy, climbing over rocks and roots, making their way along the winding trail. On and on they pushed, hacking their way up the hillside, until they reached a small clearing. There, Abrams called for a stop; the team needed to take some water and rest for a moment.

He checked his map and compass settings again. "We should be close," he said. "Keep your eyes and ears open, boys."

He then called them in close, for a quick review. "Listen up. There should be a narrow road, just ahead. When we reach it, we'll move in single file across the road, and into more cover. We'll move east, about half a klick; from there, the target should be close enough to see our flare." He looked over the serious-looking young faces and continued: "No one is to move to the target until I give the order. Check your fire; we've got brothers in arms out there, so let's do this right."

As they began to cross the road, Lieutenant Abrams heard a noise. He froze for a moment, listening closely: it sounded like a truck, heading their way. He ordered the rangers to quickly clear the road, and positioned his men in the cover, with their weapons at the ready. The last of his men was just moving into position, as a transport truck filled with rebel troops appeared from around the bend.

The driver slammed on the brakes, as if he had caught sight of them, and the truck slid sideways off of the gravel road, screeching to a halt in a cloud of dust.

Abrams gave the signal to hold fire, as the rebels piled out of the truck, heavily armed. As soon as they were within range, Abrams made the decision in a heartbeat. "Open fire!" he cried. "Fire at will!"

The brutal barrage was over in a matter of minutes. Abrams and the rangers used the element of surprise to their advantage, easily taking the rebels down, one by one, from their well-hidden place in the jungle cover. A deadly torrent of hot lead tore into the rebel troops, as they frantically tried to respond. The few who remained fled for their lives, after a rocket grenade blew up their truck.

Abrams then signaled to hold fire, and the rangers waited in the cover, until the smoke cleared.

*

"What the...?" Tex said, looking out at the road. "Did you hear that?"

Suddenly, there was intense automatic weapon-fire, followed by a ground-shaking explosion.

He scanned with the field glasses, but saw nothing in the immediate area. "There's a firefight out there, somewhere by the road we came in on!" he yelled, as he ran for a better look.

Rob turned to Beth Anne. "It has to be American troops, coming for us; it just has to be."

*

Back on the road, Abrams formed up his team. As they checked the bodies, and gathered enemy weapons and ammo, he was relieved that none of his men had been killed or injured. Wiping the blood off of his hands, he announced: "They sure were in a big hurry. We made it across and into the cover just in time. It was a perfect ambush – even if we didn't plan it. I don't doubt these rebels were coming for our people."

"Thank God we got here in time to stop them," one of the rangers added.

Abrams pointed to the pile of guns and ammo. "Disable and bury those quickly, fellas. We've got to keep moving."

*

At the ranch, Rob was once again haunted by his memories of war, this time courtesy of the firefight he had just heard.

"That's got to be our boys," Tex yelled, pacing along the fence. "They musta run into some trouble on the road. We best wait and see what happens. I don't see anything yet, but the road is not too far; be ready with that smoke, partner."

Rob had his rifle in one hand and a smoke grenade in the

other; he was ready. He didn't know who was coming, but he sensed they were close.

*

Back on the trail, Armand and the three survivors of the ambush stopped running like scared rabbits. They stopped a good distance from the ranch, in a small clearing by the trail.

Armand was in a full-on rage, his face flushed with anger as he paced back and forth looking at his men. "Again!" he screamed. "Again, I must wait for my revenge! So many more of my men killed!"

He looked toward the ranch and promised: "When I find them, I will cut out their hearts!"

He radioed to all available troops in the area, and ordered: "Get to this location, now! Bring as many men and weapons as the truck can carry."

Armand and his men all had shrapnel wounds from the blast, but that would not stop them from sneaking back to the ranch, to seek their revenge.

*

The rangers moved along the road, toward their target, with Abrams on point once again. Soon, they saw a white fence in the distance.

Abrams ordered two of his men to set up a claymore

along the road. "Stay in position and keep an eye out for trouble," he said. "I know we blasted those bastards pretty good back there, but we can't take anything for granted, and I don't want to leave our flank open. Rebels are like cockroaches: there are always more of them; they could send another truck at any time."

The rest of the team continued, following the fence along the tree line. Through his field glasses, Abrams saw what appeared to be a large ranch across an open field, with horses grazing by a stone house in the distance. He smiled, as he checked his map and compass.

"This is it. If the coordinates are correct, we should find our people here."

He gave the order, and one of the rangers fired a flare out over the field, sending a bright-red light streaming toward the ranch. Then, Abrams waited, his nerves on edge. He prayed the team would find their people alive and well.

Chapter 16
SAVIORS ABOVE

Rob couldn't help but worry; *What's going on out there? Could it be the rebels again, or is it really the good guys?* His heart lightened significantly, when a white streak flashed over the field, then popped into a bright, red flare.

Beth Anne jumped up and down, and yelled: "Look! Look! It's like the Fourth of July!"

Tex smiled. "That'll be them. Thank God."

Rob ran out of cover and threw the smoke grenade, with all of his might. It landed well away from them, in the grass, before going off with a pop. Beth Anne jumped for joy, as the yellow smoke drifted over the field. As they waited in the cover, this time Rob's hands shook from excitement and hope that, at last, his prayers had been answered.

"There, along the fence line!" Tex yelled. "They're coming for us!"

Rob grabbed the field glasses and peered through them. He began to chuckle with delight when he saw a group of soldiers moving their way, single file, along the fence. Tex lowered his rifle and called out to the troops: "We are Americans! Americans! We mean no harm. Please, help us!"

Three of the rangers now came into full view, one of

them clearly a lieutenant. The leader of the men took out a photograph as he came closer, and the tension instantly eased on his face.

"You must be Doc Marrino," he said, grabbing Rob's hand. "I'm Lieutenant Abrams. We hoped to find you still here. Looks like we got here just in time."

Flooded with relief, Rob excitedly shook the lieutenant's hand. "You guys are a sight for sore eyes. Thank God you're here!"

Abrams smiled. "We hit those rebels good; I don't think they'll be back anytime soon. How is everyone? Any wounded?"

Tex smiled as he came forward. "Yeah, but Doc and his nurse took good care of me. We woulda been outta this hellhole a long time ago, but our ride home got blown up."

Rob added: "The people who own this ranch helped us out; we freed their daughter from the cartel lockup. The rebels tried to hit us last night, but we stopped them."

As the rangers gathered around, smiles and handshakes were exchanged; everyone was relieved. Rob scanned the ranch with the field glasses and, just as he expected, saw a smiling Myia, Eduardo and Maria watching them.

"What's the game plan now, Lieutenant?" Tex asked.

As Rob and Tex discussed the details with the lieutenant, the rangers went out along the fence line to set up a defensive perimeter, before one of the men came over and handed Abrams a signal transponder, similar to the one Tex and Rob had used.

Abrams handed it to Tex: "The honor's all yours. Go ahead, turn yours off and set this one up. You would not believe how many people are on pins and needles, waiting for this signal – even the gosh-darn president! Help will be here in no time."

Rob put his arm around his wife and whispered in her ear: "Did you hear that? The president! Honey, we're going home."

She hugged him, tight. "Yes, Rob; home and the kids. I miss them so much."

Abrams received word from his men that the road was quiet, with no cartel or rebel forces in sight – good news for everybody.

*

Out at sea, Admiral Sinclair was having breakfast in his cabin when the call came in; it was the good news he had been waiting for. As soon as that call ended, he hung up, grabbed the com-link and immediately gave the order for their extraction, putting the ship on full alert. He quickly gulped down the rest of his breakfast, grabbed his hat and headed for the flight deck.

The pilots and ship-crew scrambled to get the choppers ready for take-off. Then, the officers returned a salute to the admiral, as the 'copters lifted off and lurched out over the rolling sea. As they disappeared into the sunny horizon, Sinclair headed to the bridge, ready to personally follow up on the mission with radar and radio contact.

*

Back on the ranch, after a long wait, a call came from the inbound chopper, on Abram's radio: "Bravo. Bravo. Do you copy?"

Abrams keyed his radio, as he recognized the call sign. "Copy, Bravo. Delta One is on location; we are all good and ready for extraction."

"Copy that, Delta One. We're coming your way."

Out on the coastline, the choppers came in at top speed, turned inland and followed the transponder signal coordinates.

Abrams walked around the field and ordered his men to secure a landing zone, as Tex turned off the old transponder, and watched the Rangers set up the landing perimeter. The inbound chopper cut back to half speed as they neared the target area. Rob was so filled with excitement; it seemed like an eternity before he finally heard the familiar thumping of the choppers.

Beth Anne jumped again; "Look! Look, honey; over there!"

Rob smiled. "That's them, alright," he said, watching the two choppers coming in over the treetops, fast and low.

Out on the jungle trail, Armand frantically signaled the truck to a stop. "There! Get them!" He pointed as he yelled out, "we will have revenge!"

Armand immediately dispersed his troops in the direction of the sound of the incoming choppers. As soon as the helicopters came into view above the tree line, Armand ordered his men to open fire.

"We gotta move out!" Abrams yelled, as the gunfire erupted. "Gimme some smoke!"

On command, one of the rangers stepped forward and threw a smoke grenade in the direction of the incoming choppers, sending a thick column of yellow smoke drifting over the tree line. Abrams ordered his men from the road to move toward the gunfire, so that they could help to defend the landing zone.

"Bravo! Bravo!" he yelled into his radio. "This is Delta One. Delta One. Copy? Mark my smoke. We have the L.Z. secured. Copy?"

"Copy that, Delta One," the chopper pilot confirmed. "Bravo has spotted the mark: yellow smoke. Be advised, we are receiving small-arms fire. I repeat: small-arms fire. Be prepared to board as soon as we touch down."

"Copy that, Bravo," Abrams replied,

As the lieutenant's men took defensive positions and fired toward the rebel location, the choppers hovered over the treetops, then descended on the field; grass and dust flew everywhere from the rotor wash.

Abrams ran over to Rob and pointed to one of the choppers. "It's go time for you three!" he said.

Two Rangers stood guard and followed with their weapons drawn, as Rob, Beth Anne and Tex ran toward the chopper and jumped on board.

Rob was so happy, he almost forgot how much he hated riding in the damn things. As they lifted off, he looked down and saw the brave, selfless rangers firing into the surrounding tree line.

Then, he caught the glimpse of a bright flash, heading in their direction.

The pilot saw it, too, and slammed the bird into a hard turn, just in time. The rocket streaked by, just a few feet from them, and exploded in the distance. Then, the chopper accelerated away from the field, gained altitude and leveled off.

On the ground, the rangers jumped into the second chopper, only to find themselves hit by incoming fire from the trees, courtesy of Armand and his rebels closing in. Abrams and his men returned fire, staying low as the pilot hit the throttle. The door gunner on the first chopper opened fire on the rebels, spraying cover with his 50-caliber machine gun.

Once the second chopper had lifted off and gained some altitude, its pilot rotated the aircraft in line with the trees, to unleash a barrage of cannon-fire and rockets; the enemy's position erupted into nothing more than a bright, orange-red fireball. Armand and his rebels were killed instantly by the deadly blasts.

The choppers and everyone inside them rocked back and forth wickedly from the shockwaves of the explosions; the assault was so violent that both pilots struggled to keep their aircraft under control.

Then, job done, they hit the throttle and accelerated away from the hell below.

"Wow, Doc! That rocket was mighty close!" Tex chuckled, nervously.

"Yeah, too close," Rob agreed. He was so relieved that the rangers had made it safely onto the chopper behind them, he thanked God, as he held Beth Anne close.

"Everybody okay back there?" a member of the flight crew asked, as they all settled into their seats.

"We're fine," Beth Anne said, with a shaky voice, and an expression of fatigue and worry etched onto her face. A dislike of helicopters was something she had in common with her husband, and the near-miss of the rocket had frightened the hell out of her.

"Good," said the pilot, calm and reassuring. "Everything is being arranged from the carrier, and there's a jet waiting for you there, to take you back to a Florida Air Force base."

The noise and vibration settled down, as the chopper reached cruising speed. Soon, everyone was lulled into a comfortable silence, thrilled that their nightmare was almost over.

On the second chopper, Abrams was more than happy to be making the call to Admiral Sinclair. "Com One, this is Delta One. Copy?"

Still standing on the ship's bridge, Sinclair grabbed the mic: "We copy, Delta One. Do you have the package?"

Abrams smiled. "Roger, Com One; the package is secure.

We are inbound, coming in on your southeast."

"Copy that, Delta One: from the southeast. We'll be expecting you."

As soon as Sinclair put down the mic, the whole bridge erupted in cheers; everyone on board was obviously relieved. The admiral ordered the immediate launch of two fighter jets, to provide escort for the incoming choppers, and the flight deck came to life, as crews and pilots scrambled for take-off.

Within a matter of minutes, the carrier turned into the wind, and the jets were on their way. Immediately, Sinclair went to his quarters, to make a very important call of his own.

*

In Washington, the president was just finishing his morning cabinet meeting, when the call came in.

He rose from his seat and, with a broad smile on his face, happily announced: "Ladies and gentlemen, I am thrilled to report that our Colombian situation is over; the extraction was successful and our people are en route back home, with no casualties to report."

He sat back down, took a sigh and a sip of coffee, then continued: "I want to extend my personal congratulations to all involved in this delicate mission. In cooperation with the Colombian government, we have dealt a major blow to the cartel and the rebel terrorists. This will go down as a victory in the war on drugs, and I want the American people to know about it: as soon as they arrive home safely, issue a press release."

The room filled with cheers and handshakes; so many had been waiting and praying for good news about the lost Americans. It only took minutes for the news to start its trickle through the grapevine.

*

On the inbound chopper, the pilot radioed the carrier one last time, to make sure they were clear for landing. Then, he turned to his passengers: "E.T.A. less than ten minutes."

Filled with emotion, Beth Anne finally let go of her fear and hugged Rob tightly, crying tears of joy. The whole experience had been unspeakably rough on her, but the thought of being back in her homeland, and seeing her children again, warmed her heart.

Tex smiled, as he looked at the two of them. "Looks like we made it in and out of Hell again, Doc."

"You got that right, my friend. I had my doubts when that first chopper blew – thank God we weren't on it."

They were all happy, but exhausted, their bodies having run on fear and adrenalin for days. For a moment, the relaxation caught up, and Rob drifted off; his mind traveled back in time to 'Nam, and that same feeling of relief when being lifted out of a hot L.Z.

"Rob, I didn't think I'd ever see you or the kids again,"

Beth Anne said, snapping him out of it. "That general and his men were pigs; they tried to rape us. It was horrible..." She paused to let her sobs escape, then softly continued: "God bless both of you; you risked everything to save our lives. And now, finally, we're going home. I miss my children so much it hurts."

Rob kissed her tear-stained cheeks. "I know. I prayed for this day, and I did my best; the good Lord and Tex did the rest." As Rob held her, in that moment he felt a flood of relief, as if a giant weight had been lifted from his shoulders.

Tex jerked back from the window when the awesome sight of a sleek fighter jet came into view. "Looks like we got a little company, Doc."

Rob and Beth Anne watched in awe as another jet came into view, on their side of the aircraft.

"Looks like we're getting the F-15 red-carpet treatment today, folks," the pilot said, over the loudspeaker.

Rob smiled and looked at his friend. "You know something? I've always wanted to fly in one of those jets." Then, he pondered; "But, I think I've had enough excitement for now."

Tex smiled, happy for his friend and his lady. "You think so?"

Chapter 17
THE NEWS

At the Air Force command center, General Jaskins was with Base Commander Simson, when the call came in from the commander-in-chief.

The president thanked the general, saying that he was proud of the successful mission, and wanted to thank everyone personally. Jaskins shared the great news with Simson, and they shared an elated handshake.

Full of excitement, Jaskins left for his quarters and made some calls, summoning everyone to a special meeting at six p.m. Joyfully, he decided on a fresh shirt and a quick shave, before meeting Simson and some friends for a celebratory lunch.

Later that evening, Jaskins went back to his office and grabbed his briefcase. He was running a little late for the big meeting, and he ordered his aide to bring the Jeep around, for the trip across the base to the command center.

General Jaskins entered the planning room with a big smile on his face, as he looked around him at the suits and military brass. Anyone who knew him could see right away that there was a new spring in his step; Agent Sanders spotted it right away.

He must have a damn good reason for being in such a

good mood, she thought. She'd had her doubts about the mission all along, but now, Sanders could feel in her bones, her prayers had been answered.

Too excited to sit, Jaskins paced at the head of the conference table and called the meeting to order. "Ladies and gentlemen, I have spoken with the president, and we have very good news indeed. Before I share it with you, please remember that this information is highly confidential and must remain secure, until we have official confirmation that the mission is fully complete. The rescue team has found our people alive and well."

A flood of relief overwhelmed the room, and everyone cheered and applauded for the good news. When the crowd had settled down, Jaskins continued: "There was heavy resistance from the cartel and rebel forces, but it has been neutralized. We have been successful in all of our endeavors, and it appears that none of our people were killed or seriously wounded. The group was picked up at an undisclosed landing zone in Colombia, and are currently on their way back to a Navy carrier, off the coast. The president is very happy, and has asked me to let everyone know that we should all be proud of a job well done."

Again, the group broke out in cheers and accolades. Enjoying his moment of fame and glory, General Jaskins shook hands with everyone around the table.

Relieved, Agent Sanders left the meeting with a few close co-workers in tow, ready to head to the officers' club, for a drink to celebrate the occasion.

*

Back in New Jersey, Chief Roy was slumped over in his old, leather office chair. The ringing phone startled him out of his daydream. He was surprised to hear Agent Sanders's voice on the other end.

"Chief," she said, "I have some very good news for you: Rob and Beth Anne are on their way home. Everyone is okay."

Roy almost fell backward, as he jumped out of his chair, suddenly wide awake. "They're okay?! Dear God! Really? Wh-where are they?" he asked, suddenly out of breath. "When will we see them?"

"They're on their way home as we speak. I don't have any more details at this time, but I'm sure we will hear from them soon. Please keep this under your hat, Chief; immediate family only, until further notice."

Roy was so excited he could hardly speak, but he managed to thank her, before hanging up the phone.

He ran for his jacket and fumbled through all of the paraphernalia on his desk, until he found his keys. "Mind the shop while I'm gone!" he yelled to the front desk officer, as he bolted out the door. "I'll be back tomorrow."

Lawman or not, Roy broke every speed limit, as he drove like a maniac to Bill and Susan's house.

Bill sensed something was up the moment Roy jumped out of his car with that ridiculous, clownish grin on his face.

"What's going on? What is it?" he asked.

"Bill, by God, they made it!" Roy shouted. "They're all okay, and they'll be home soon! We should hear more in a few hours."

Bill couldn't believe his ears. "Jesus! Good Lord! They made it. Are you sure?"

Roy pulled Bill into a brotherly hug. "Yeah, one-hundred percent; I just got word from the F.B.I. We've gotta keep it under wraps for now; immediate family only."

Bill smiled. "Come on in and have some coffee. We can share the good news together."

Bill and Roy found Susan so distracted by making dinner, she didn't even notice Roy smiling at her, until she turned toward the table. "Oh!" she said, startled. "Roy, why didn't you tell me we were having your company for dinner?"

Bill walked over to her, with an enormous smile on his face, unable to keep the secret for even a moment; "Honey, they made it! Roy just got word."

"What?" she asked, her eyes growing wide.

"Rob and our Beth Anne... They're on their way home!"

Susan was as still as a statue, just staring at Roy's face until the words sank in. When she started to understand what she was being told, her face lit up, and she nearly dropped the casserole dish she was holding. "My God! Our prayers have been answered! I have to go tell the kids!"

She smiled and put the food on the table; "Well, uh, it is time for dinner, so... Look, just help yourselves!" Roy smiled as she then scurried off, muttering to herself.

The men dug into their dinner, listening to the sounds of joy echoing down the stairs; the laughter and happiness warmed their souls as much as the food warmed their bellies.

Chapter 18
HOMECOMING

Off the northern coast of Colombia, all hands were on deck, awaiting the arrival of the rescue team. Admiral Sinclair and his staff stood on the bridge, with their eyes on the radar, tracking the choppers as they flew closer. After a while, the admiral went out on the stairwell and scanned the sky with his long-range scope; he was thrilled to spot them on the southeast horizon. Full of excitement, they then left the bridge to head for the flight deck.

"There it is, Doc!" Tex shouted in the helicopter, first to see the giant carrier slicing through the rolling waves.

Beth looked out into the ocean, then back at Rob, with a worried look in her eyes. "We're supposed to land on that thing?"

Tex smiled. "It won't be no problem at all, missy; don't fret. Just close your eyes and it will all be over 'fore ya know it. These guys do this stuff all the time."

"Yeah, we'll be fine, honey," Rob tried to reassure her, even though he wasn't too crazy about the idea himself. Truth be told, his stomach was in knots, as the chopper began its descent toward the rocking carrier deck.

Admiral Sinclair watched with pride, as his flight crew guided the choppers onto the flight deck, expertly. As soon as the whirlybirds touched down, he and his staff rushed over to greet the passengers. Rob and Tex were helping Beth Anne out as he approached. Sinclair smiled broadly and grabbed Rob's hand. "Welcome aboard! It's good to have you back."

Lieutenant Abrams stepped forward and saluted. "Everyone is present and accounted for, sir," he announced.

"That's good news, indeed," Sinclair said. He turned back to Tex: "Let's go below deck; it's more comfortable down there."

Rob took his wife's hand and followed the admiral. Walking felt strange to both of them, as the deck swayed slightly under their feet.

Once below, they were escorted to the medical room, where the staff gave them a once-over. The doctor instructed Tex to lie down on a cot, so he could check his wound, while Rob and Beth Anne were presented with clean clothes by the admiral's staff, before they were escorted downstairs, to their quarters.

"Look, Rob, we've even got our own private shower!" Beth Anne squealed, when they were alone.

Rob just smiled, lying on his bunk and watching his wife undress. He felt heat growing inside him, as she slipped into the shower. But, he quickly put those ideas out of his head. *There will plenty of time for that back home,* he told himself.

When Beth Anne returned, she was dressed in a baggy, blue jumpsuit, though she still looked wonderful. "Oh Rob, the hot shower feels so good. You've gotta get in there."

Rob didn't have to be told twice.

As he was undressing, he heard a knock at the door.

"Hey, Doc," Tex said from the other side.

Rob opened the door and Tex smiled, standing there in a clean jumpsuit of his own – although, his bulky physique filled it out much more than Beth Anne's feminine figure did.

"Admiral says we need to meet in half an hour," Tex told him, "but, uh... you ain't plannin' to go in your skivvies, are ya?"

Rob laughed. "Listen, buddy, if you keep talking, I just might have to. We'll meet you topside in twenty minutes."

Beth Anne joined Tex in a long laugh, as Rob ran into the bathroom; they both agreed that it was good to laugh again, especially at Rob's expense.

Admiral Sinclair ordered the ship to full speed, on a due-north heading toward the U.S. mainland. As soon as he saw that his orders had been heard, he left the bridge and got ready to meet with his new guests.

Rob, Beth Anne and Tex met up as planned, and followed an escort to the meeting room, where Sinclair and his staff were already assembled. It was a well-furnished place, with a large table in the center.

After everyone took their seats, Sinclair stood at the head of the table, and smiled as he spoke: "I hope you find your quarters comfortable. If you need anything at all, just ask."

Rob stood up. "Admiral, we can't thank you and the

Rangers enough. I don't think we would have made it without you."

"You're most welcome," the admiral replied humbly, as Rob resumed his seat. "I'm damn proud of my crew, and all those who helped to make the rescue mission successful. As for now, I think you will have a smoother flight if you get some sleep and disembark first thing in the morning. Everything has already been arranged for your safe departure; we're heading home at full speed."

"Sounds good to me," Tex said; "I think we've all had enough excitement for one day."

"I think we can all agree with that!" the admiral said, while Beth Anne and Rob nodded. "Dinner will be delivered to your quarters within the hour. I hope you all have a good night."

After dinner, Rob and Beth Anne went up onto the deck, with what was left of the wine, to get some air.

Rob poured the wine and took out his Cuban cigar. He lit it up and took a slow drag. "Man, that's good!" he said, as he watched the smoke puff out over the sea.

Beth Anne smiled. "Where did you get that?"

"From a sailboat captain we met, on our way to find you," he replied, with a smile.

They looked out, at the endless miles of rolling ocean, and talked about home. Afterward, they went below and finished the last of the wine.

What then started as a goodnight kiss ended a good while later...

Basking in the afterglow, they fell asleep to the gentle rocking of the ship.

*

The next morning broke, calm and clear, and the mighty carrier began the day by turning into the wind.

Tex, already sitting by the plane and smoking a Marlboro, spotted Rob and Beth Anne, as soon as they ventured onto the flight deck. "Looks like we got us a nice little jet to ride in this time," he said, waving them over.

Rob smiled. "That's a good thing; I don't think either of us can take another chopper ride."

Beth Anne laughed: "Amen to that; no choppers."

The pilots came out of the cockpit, and proceeded to show them around the twin-engine jet, which boasted a shiny, navy-blue paint job and a comfortable leather interior.

"You all take it easy now," Admiral Sinclair said, as he and his staff walked over to see them off, with well wishes and handshakes. "Have a safe flight."

"Thank you, sir," Tex replied, with a smile.

Lieutenant Abrams and two of his rangers boarded the aircraft in full gear, occupying the rear seats. "We're your official escorts," he explained; "the mission is not considered complete until you are safely back on U.S. soil."

"That's fine," Rob replied, as they shook hands; "we're lucky to have you."

Before long, everyone was on board and buckled in, the jet's engines warmed up and ready for take-off. The aircraft slowly began to roll down the flight deck, where it was guided into its final position by the flagman. Finally, everyone on deck waved, as he dropped the flag and gave them the go signal.

The pilot slowly raised the throttle, while holding the brakes; the plane vibrated and the roar of the engines surged. Then, as the pilot released the brakes, it thrust down the deck, pinning everyone inside to their seats, from the force of the acceleration. In a blur, the aircraft leapt off of the end of the carrier, dropped very slightly toward the water, before climbing steeply and gaining altitude. Rob looked over at Beth Anne, only to find her squeezing her eyes shut; she looked as if she were riding the world's scariest rollercoaster. Finally, the pilot backed off the throttle, and the plane began to level off.

"Whoo-whee!" Tex yelled. "That was one helluva ride!"

"Good God, I hope I never have to do that again," Beth Anne said, as her husband joined her in breathing a sigh of relief.

"Yeah, that is weird!" Lieutenant Abrams chimed in. "That was the first time – and hopefully the last – for me; we usually ride in choppers."

The pilots laughed, and one teased over his shoulder: "Oh, come on, guys. It wasn't that bad, was it?"

Before long, they were all laughing and joking about the experience.

During the flight, Abrams told them everything he knew about the people involved in the operation; "Lots of cogs and wheels had to be in place on this one, folks, from the president on downwards."

"'Operation Sledgehammer', huh?" Tex smiled. "Can you believe that, Rob? I knew we'd be famous someday."

Rob laughed. "It's been one hell of an experience, my friend, but I'm not looking for fortune and glory. In fact, I plan to tell everyone it was just you, the big Texan, who came to the rescue. Beth Anne and I just want to go home, to be with our kids."

Beth Anne added: "He's right, Tex; you'll always be my hero."

"Gee, thanks," Tex said, sheepishly, miming a tip of his hat.

As they continued teasing Tex, the co-pilot walked into the cabin and opened a large case, revealing a wonderful array of food and drinks. "Help yourselves," he said.

After their snacks, they all settled down for the trip, lullabied into silence by the low humming of the jet engines. Beth Anne drifted off, pondering her good fortune for escaping that dreadful place.

*

Somewhere over the Gulf of Mexico, the plane began its slow turn and descent – a change in movement which stirred Rob from his nap. He looked over at Tex and saw that he was still snoozing; Beth Anne was busy reading the paper.

"You know," Beth Anne said, peeking over the top of the newspaper at him, "you guys ought to compete in a loudest snoring contest someday."

Rob looked at Tex, sprawled out on his seat. "Since when? I don't sound anything like that buzz-saw!"

"I beg to differ," she teased.

Abrams smiled. "The lady is right, my man. I put my earplugs in after the first five minutes."

As they laughed, Rob checked his watch. "Wow, I've been out for almost two hours!"

"Yeah, but I think we're landing soon," Beth Anne said, putting her paper down in her lap: "we've been descending slowly for the past ten minutes. I hope that's on purpose."

Rob laughed. "I'm sure it is, honey. We're almost home."

Tex, now awakened by their talking, stretched and looked out of the window, into the puffy, white clouds. "Are we there yet?"

"We're landing soon," Rob said.

"There's still some coffee and sandwiches, if you'd like any," Abrams offered.

"A cuppajo sounds good right about now," Tex replied. Then, he turned quizzically to Abrams;

"Hey, Lieutenant, if ya don't mind my askin', what's your first name? I don't feel like I can thank ya proper 'til I know it."

"It's Francis, but my friends call me Frank," Abrams replied, as he sat next to them, holding the coffee tray.

Tex shook his hand. "Well, thanks Frank. You and your boys did a helluva job getting us out of that place."

"Roger that, Frank," Rob added; "you pulled us out just in the nick of time."

Abrams smiled. "You have just as much to be proud of: what you two did was incredible. You went in there, put a good hit on that cartel and pulled off a rescue on your own. It's really unbelievable."

Beth Anne smiled. "It is, and I'm so grateful and proud of both of them. That cartel would have killed me, I'm sure," she said, instantly losing her smile.

"Well, ma'am, I'm glad we got out clean, with no one lost or wounded. Everything seemed to fall into place for us; we found ourselves in the right place at the right time." Abrams sipped his coffee and continued: "Those rebels in the truck would've been a big problem for everyone – thank God we got the jump on them. From the looks of it, the base is gone, and add to that the number of rebels killed... well, I think we've put that particular cartel out of business for a long time."

"We heard the firefight," Rob said. "It was pretty tense, waiting there and not knowing what was going on."

"Well, we were worried about you as well," Abrams said. "Sure, it's a ranger's job to answer the call, but I think most of us would've gone in, even without the orders. We've heard about you two, and the things you did to save our boys, years ago. This mission was an honor; a chance to help veterans in need. In fact, over a hundred soldiers volunteered for it."

His words caught Rob by surprise. "Over a hundred? Really."

"Really."

"Wow! 'Nam was a long time ago, but it's good to know that some people remember we did do *some* good."

"That's really what it's all about, boys," Tex said: "fighting with your brothers, to shine a light into the darkness of evil. Rob and I just... well, let's just say we did what had to be done."

"We are a go for approach," the pilot interrupted, over the intercom. "Everyone fasten those seatbelts and prepare for landing."

The Air Force base was abuzz, as the jet made its smooth landing and taxied off of the runway.

The moment they stepped off the plane, a group of officers greeted them with smiles and handshakes. Tex instantly fell to his knees and kissed the ground. "God bless America!" he shouted.

General Jaskins stepped forward, returning the salutes of Abrams and his mighty rangers. "Welcome back, everyone, and congratulations on a job well done."

He then walked over to Rob, Tex and Beth Anne; "We're sure glad to see you three."

"Please, please come this way," advised Air Force Commander Simson; "we've got a lot to talk about."

In the background, a long line of soldiers stood at attention and saluted, as the group walked by. They followed Simson into a large van, for the quick trip across the sprawling airfield.

The massive red-brick and gray metal command center soon came into view, and the driver pulled over at the main entrance, to let the group out. Simpson stopped for a moment, giving orders to his men, while Rob, Beth Anne and Tex continued toward the doorway.

"Welcome home!" said Agent Sanders, greeting them at the front entrance, with a pretty smile. She came forward and reached for Rob's hand. "I'm so pleased to see all of you alive and well."

"Thanks for all your help," Rob said, gladly taking her offered hand.

"Yeah, your intel was right on the money," Tex added, with a smile.

After Agent Sanders walked away, Beth Anne looked curiously at Rob. "Who's she?"

"F.B.I. agent," Rob replied. "She gave us the top-secret information on the cartel base, which helped us to find you."

"Oh, because for a moment there, I thought she was... never mind," she winked. "I need to thank her personally; I'll give her a call when we get back."

An assistant from the commander's staff greeted them, and led them to private quarters, for a little downtime. They were thankful to get out of the jumpsuits and into better clothes, which were sized just right – right down to the sneakers. They also appreciated the kind gesture of baskets of fresh fruit in their rooms.

*

Beth Anne was munching on an apple and watching T.V. when the phone rang. She couldn't help laughing when Rob ran out of the bathroom to answer it, losing his towel in the process.

"There will be a debriefing," the general's aide told, and it was all Rob could do to keep from laughing, as he looked down at his naked bottom half; *You can say that again!* The aide continued, informing him: "An escort will arrive for you within the hour."

When the escort arrived, Rob and Beth Anne followed him down a long hallway, to a set of enormous, brass-trimmed oak double-doors. General Jaskins and Commander Simson greeted them, as they entered the planning room. "Come and sit," Jaskins smiled. "We have a few details to go over."

Tex smiled at Rob, as the two of them looked around the impressive room, immaculately decorated and chock-full of military brass. Everyone had smiles for them, as they took their seats alongside Lieutenant Abrams and his rangers.

From the head of the table, Jaskins said: "Congratulations, ladies and gentlemen; kudos on one hell of an operation! A job well done by everyone." He smiled at Beth Anne, as he continued: "The president sends his regards, and has asked me to tell you he's relieved you're back on American soil. If there is anything you need while you're here, please let us know; it is our pleasure to do anything we can for you."

Rob looked at Tex before he spoke, and his happy face said everything. "Well sir, first I want to thank you and everyone in this room; the flight crew who came in hot and pulled us out did an outstanding job. In addition, I am eternally grateful for the heroic actions of Lieutenant Abrams and his team; without their support, we would not have made it out of a very bad situation. Now, we just want to go home, to our kids, and forget this nightmare ever happened."

Tex added: "We were doin' okay on our own, but once that chopper was blown to bits... well, after that I had my doubts we'd ever see home again. For that reason, I also have to thank y'all; as you said, it was a helluva mission! Those cartel bastards won't be bothering anyone for a long time. My friends and I are lookin' forward to getting back to our lives, and none of us are interested in headlines or money; that was not what any of this was about."

Jaskins smiled and nodded. "Understood," he said. "But, you should know that the story broke this morning; after your plane left the carrier, the president called a news conference: he praised the men of Bravo and Delta teams, and the success of the operation – another battle won in our country's war on drugs. Nothing much was mentioned about your rescue plan, except that you were held captive and rescued by U.S. forces, in a daring attack on the cartel."

"Sounds good to me, sir," Tex replied.

"I agree," Rob said, with a nod; "we'd prefer to stay out of the limelight as much as possible."

"Well," Jaskins replied, "we'll do our best to protect you from all that, but I'm sure some press will linger for a while. I'll leave those details to Agent Sanders and her people."

*

Back home in Pikesville, Chief Roy was thrilled when the call came in.

"Hey, Chief, our party's coming home!" Agent Sanders gleefully announced. "Rob and Beth Anne should arrive at the airport around five p.m.; I suggest you be there at least half an hour early. I'll give you more details as they become available."

"Oh, that's wonderful news!" Roy replied. "We'll all be waiting for them. Thank you so much, and God bless you for all of your help."

Roy hung up the phone, and sat back to revel in the moment himself, before excitedly dialing Bill and Susan.

*

There was a smile of relief pasted onto Agent Sanders's face, as she hung up the phone. Of all the cases she had handled, this was the most emotional for her; she knew she had allowed herself to get a little too close to Rob, and to develop feelings for him and his children. She had seen so many similar cases go horribly wrong, and she prayed his would turn out differently. *Thank God it did!* she thought.

It was a warm, reassuring feeling, to realize that she had finally made a difference in the world – even if only on this one case.

*

It was early-afternoon at the airbase, and everyone was ready to depart. Beth Anne and Rob would catch a flight home, but Tex was going to travel by car. "I'm gonna drive north to Orlando and meet up with the family," he explained; "have us a little vacation, before we head back on down to the ranch."

Then, Tex gave Rob a nod and pointed to the doorway. They walked outside and found a quiet, out-of-the-way spot, where Tex reached into his pack and pulled out a heavy, black, nylon sack, which he handed to his buddy.

Rob's eyes widened as he looked inside; "Wow, man! How much is in here?"

"Just your half, my friend," Tex replied with a smirk: "about a hundred grand in assorted bills. Plus, since we got my target, I'll be sending a little more cash, to cover the trip. Just let the money lie low for a little while; tell no one but your missus about it."

"How do I let this much money lie low?" Rob asked, looking at him, dubiously. "I can't exactly hide it in a shoebox, under the bed."

Tex laughed. "Well, you could. But, I'll do ya one better: I've got a reliable contact, with an offshore bank; I'll give him your number, when I call him to set up my account. Don't worry: he is very good, and I trust him. He'll arrange everything."

Rob stared at the money again, in disbelief. "I had no idea Eduardo gave us this much. Are you sure you took your full share, Tex?"

Tex smiled, as he lit up a Marlboro. "Oh, don't you worry 'bout me, Doc; I'm in for a big payday, for that hit on the rebel general."

"Good; you deserve it, my friend." Rob smiled as they shook hands, "thanks, I can't believe how this has all turned out: I got my love back, and a nice bonus, to boot. Anyway, we'd better get back inside, before someone comes looking for us."

"Can we really keep that much?" Beth Anne whispered, after Rob and Tex pulled her aside and told her about the unexpected paycheck.

"Why not?" Rob replied, with a shrug. "It's better in our hands than in the hands of that evil cartel. It'll give the kids a good start in life, and we can even make a nice donation to the church, or a charity."

"That's great." Beth Anne pulled him into a tight hug. "Now, can we please go home to our babies?"

Tex smiled. "I like the charity idea. That's sorta what it was in the first place: a donation to us, for savin' Myia's life. As far as I'm concerned, that money doesn't even exist."

"What money?" Rob added, as he regretfully let go of his wife and embraced his friend.

Tex laughed. "For the record, Doc, we're even now – as long as nobody gets hijacked again!"

"We'll always be more than even, Tex," Rob replied; "I am yours anytime, anywhere, my friend."

A shiny, black limousine pulled up, and the driver got out and opened the passenger door.

"I can get my own bags," Tex told the chauffeur. He then turned to Rob and Beth Anne; "Looks like my ride's here, and they got me traveling first class. See you guys soon. Call me when you get home, so we can plan a celebration – maybe a big party at my ranch."

Beth Anne gave him a hug and thanked him again, as Rob helped him to load his gear. Then, off Tex went, with a smile and a wave.

Soon, a van pulled up to the curb, and Rob and Beth Anne climbed inside, for their short trip to the airfield.

They gave Lieutenant Abrams and his rangers a friendly wave, before they boarded the white Boeing aircraft – a luxurious private jet, compliments of the president.

One the ride home, they talked about what it would be like to get back to work, and put the whole nightmarish ordeal behind them. They decided it was best to tell the children the truth about what had happened. But, mostly, they could not wait to see them; to hold them in their arms again; to just be home and together.

"So, besides charity, the church and maybe some tuition, what are we going to do with all that cash? I mean, we can't just put it in the bank, can we?"

Rob smiled. "No, no, we have to be careful; definitely no crazy spending. I don't know about you, but I've always been happy with our life as it is. I guess, first, I'll pay back what I had to take out to fund the trip; then, after a while, we can add some to the college fund; maybe, in a few months, we can vacation in some tropical paradise."

"Just nowhere in South America," Beth Anne said, then winced.

"Absolutely not," Rob agreed, with a grin. "As for the rest of the cash, we can keep it in an offshore account."

"Sounds good to me. I love the vacation idea; Lord knows we need it."

A funny idea came to him, as he looked at her smiling face. "You're right, as usual, honey. You know, I knew there was a reason we rescued you: it was for the money! That's all we were after, right from the start of this mess."

Beth Anne's face tightened into a glare, but she couldn't hold the expression for long; in an instant, she burst out in laughter. The two of them then lovingly teased and joked with each other until their stomachs ached. Rob loved that; he always thought she looked like an angel when she smiled.

After a while, Beth Anne fell asleep on his shoulder, and Rob dozed off to the gentle rocking of the plane, blanketed by feelings of peace and warmth he didn't think he would ever experience again. He couldn't believe how well things had turned around. The fear and worry were gone, and there was joy and gratitude in their place. He was finally calm and happy.

"Fasten your seatbelts, folks; we're preparing for approach," the pilot announced over the loudspeaker.

Both of them jolted awake in excitement.

Chapter 19
HOME AT LAST

Roy had diligently written down every detail, when Agent Sanders called to tell him the flight information. She sounded as happy as he was, that all had worked out well for Rob and Beth Anne. Full of excitement, Roy scrambled to find his keys, then practically ran out of the police station, so that he could go home to shower. He put on his dress uniform and shone his shoes, then grabbed a fresh cup of coffee on the way out.

Bill, Susan and the kids were ready for the long ride to the airport; Roy had cleaned out his police cruiser to make room for everyone. He couldn't believe all the junk he had stored, on and underneath the seats. The instant he pulled up to the house, everyone quickly piled into the car, fastening their seatbelts.

After an hour of smooth sailing on the interstate, Roy reached the exit which led to Newark Airport. It had been almost a decade since he'd last been there, and he couldn't believe how much the city and the airport had grown. It took him a while to weave through the heavy traffic and find the lane for short-term parking.

After parking the car, they boarded a shuttle bus, to carry them to their terminal. Inside, they checked the incoming flight numbers and rode up a long escalator – something the kids enjoyed very much. All the while, they were laughing and squealing with excitement; Mom and Dad were finally coming home. Full of anticipation, they waited at the right gate, knowing that the waiting and the worrying would all soon be over.

*

On the plane, Rob and Beth Anne held hands, as the Boeing made its last turn, to line up for landing. The plane hovered over the runway, its nose up, then gently touched down. Beth Anne was so excited, she couldn't stay in her seat as the plane taxied toward the terminal.

The unbelievable circle of emotions they had both been through in recent weeks was not quite complete: there was still *joy* to be had. Rob thanked God for a safe landing, and for getting them to this day he had hoped and prayed for.

The plane pulled up to the terminal and shut down. Then, the co-pilot escorted them out of the plane, led them to the terminal's entrance and directed them to their gate. Quickly, they made their way down the seemingly never-ending corridor.

"Over there!" Rob said, pointing when he saw Roy smiling and waving at them. Before he could say another word, his wife had broken into a wild run toward her children.

"My babies! My babies!" Beth Anne shouted, at a full

sprint, with her arms flung wide open.

For Rob, nothing else existed in that moment, but those happy faces, the hugs, the kisses and the tears of joy. At last, they were all together; a whole family again.

After everyone settled down enough to think straight, the group made their way out of the gate, heading downstairs to catch another shuttle to the parking area. As they exited the terminal and walked toward the waiting shuttle, Rob noticed a news-van parked ahead of them.

"A statement?" a reporter begged, hurrying toward him, with camera operator in tow. "Can tell us anything about the mission? Please, Officer Marrino?"

"Maybe later," Rob said.

"Just a few words?" she pressed, nearly ramming the *Channel 7* microphone in his face.

With a sigh, Rob stepped forward. "Alright, but this will be short and sweet; one question."

The journalist smiled, happy to get the scoop before anyone else. "How do you feel to be free and with your family again?"

As the camera zoomed in on Rob, he struggled to find the right words.

"It's hard to describe how much love and joy is in my heart right now," he said, glancing over at the happy face of his wife. "I just thank God for America and for our president. I thank my dear friend and brother, Tex. We owe our lives to the U.S. military, and..." he trailed off for a moment, on the verge of tears, "...I will be forever grateful to

Lieutenant Abrams, and the rangers who risked all for our freedom, and for giving me my life, for her!"

Made in the USA
Columbia, SC
24 September 2023